I0727278

OPERATION WRATH OF SALADIN

BY MARK WROBEL

OPERATION WRATH OF SALADIN

BY: MARK WROBEL

Operation Wrath of Saladin

By Mark Wrobel

Cover Created & Designed by Isaac Brown III

Logo Designs by Andre M. Saunders/Jess Zimmerman

Editor: Anelda Lukesia Attaway

ACKNOWLEDGMENT

First and foremost, I acknowledge God and thank Him for sustaining me through life with my disability.

DEDICATION

I dedicate this book to my father Roman Wrobel who I love dearly. Also to my dear friends Carl, Chris, Amber, and Carla.

TABLE OF CONTENTS

INTRODUCTION

Yet another great book from the author Mark Wrobel, Operation Wrath of Saladin. This book takes place during current events in the Middle East. It will take you on a wild ride through the Middle East America and back to the Middle East again.

This book does contain intricate love, action, and adventure; however, it contains some current events, but it is based strictly on fiction.

CHAPTER 1

The Mission

The month was April 9, 2016, and the time was 5:15 a.m. I was sleeping in my bed in a big mansion in Virginia, and at about that time, my phone rang.

The voice on the other side of the phone was my boss, Mike, from the CIA. He said, "Mark, we need you to come in to work early today because we have a special assignment that we have to brief you on. We want you to start training and we will need you to be at work by 7 o'clock this morning instead of your 9 a.m. usual time."

"It's a little bit early for me but okay boss, I will see you there by 7 a.m., trust me, I'll be there."

I went down the stairs through my living room, and into the kitchen to fix myself some breakfast, which consisted of, one of my favorite breakfast sandwiches and a cup of coffee with milk. After breakfast, I went to take a quick shower, and I was ready for a 45-minute drive to Langley Virginia, where I worked.

For this drive this morning, I chose one of the two cars that I had in my house car garage. I am a proud owner of a McLaren, and a bright red 1986 Lamborghini Countach. the drive to work was uneventful since I left my house at 6 a.m., and I did manage to arrive at work, right at 7 a.m. on the dot. I was sitting down at my desk when my aide, Naseem, knocked on my office door and said, "Mike, the Director of Operations for the Middle Eastern section of the CIA, wants to see you in his office ASAP." One minute after Naseem, my aide, delivered the message, my phone rang. I picked up the phone and Mike said, "Mark, you were supposed to report to my office like, five minutes ago."

"Yes Sir, I'm on my way. My aide, Naseem, just delivered your message that you wanted to see me."

Naseem was working as my aide and my secretary. Mike was in charge of the Middle East section and he was a director of this particular section in the CIA. However, I was the deputy director of the Special Operations Division of the Central Intelligence Agency. Naseem was very tall, with dark hair, and dark eyes and she had long nails painted with pink nail polish. She always wore a miniskirt to work, a pantsuit, and a dark jacket; she kinda looks like Cleopatra, however, she looked two times better than that.

As I got on the elevator, I hit the sixth-floor button and walked to Mike's office. I asked, "Sir, you wanted to see me?"

"Yes, Mark, please come in and sit down. Can I offer you a drink, a Diet Coke, or a cup of coffee?"

"No thank you, Sir. What's on your mind?"

"Well, the National Security Council, with the cooperation of the Central Intelligence Agency, has put together an operation, so that we can listen and take photographs of the meeting of the President of the United States and the Prime Minister of Israel.

"Mike is spying on Israel. A no-no topic in the U.S. in general and is it even legal for the U.S. to spy on Israel?" I asked.

"You are correct in this instant; however, because they have spied and they do perform industrial espionage on us then in our case there's no reason that we cannot spy on them right back. All countries do this, you know that," Mr. Mark replied.

"Yes, I know that Sir."

Then I asked him, "What do you have in mind, Mike?"

As he sat behind his desk, he opened one of the desk drawers and pulled out a folder with the letters TOP-SECRET. He said, "There Mark have a look at it.

As I opened the folder, there was the cover page of the operation with the CIA logo and over the top of the logo, the title read Operation Wrath of Saladin. In that operation, we were to take a modified King Air Aircraft with highly sophisticated radios and computers, so that we could listen to what the President of the United States and the Prime Minister of Israel were talking about. So in that case, the U.S. would pick up some useful intelligence. That's what was written in the documentation that my boss Mike handed me in the operational folder.

So I asked Mike, "Did you already pick the team, who is supposed to carry out this operation?"

"Yes, I did. It's going to be you, Captain Ken, and the two pilots will be Lieutenant Commander Christopher and Lieutenant Commander Carl. Would you like to have a look at their files?"

"Yes Sir, I would like to take a look at them," I said to him.

It was 10:30 a.m., as I looked at those files. I looked at Carl's file first, and it read: Graduate of the Naval Academy, attended flight training school in Pensacola, Florida, graduated with honors, and completed an associate degree in International Relations from the University of Miami. I also looked at Chris's file, and it read the same as Carl's, except it said on there that Chris did a stint in juvie for truly minor infractions. I also read Captain Ken's file, which was an interesting read. He entered the U.S. Naval service right after 9/11, graduated from radio school in Texas, and did two tours of duty in Kuwait and Iraq attached to the U.S. Embassy as a defense attaché to the Central Intelligence Agency.

As we finished our coffee I told my boss, Mike I said, "I know these men, with Carl and Chris I grew up with them in the same hometown of Wilmington Delaware, and with Commander Ken, I served with him for five years in the same Navy Intelligence Unit."

"I thought that you would be familiar with those men," my boss Mike said, "That is why I picked them to help us carry out this operation."

"Okay, when does the National Security Council want us to start to carry out the Operation Wrath of Saladin?" I replied.

Well, as Mike took off his glasses and took a sip of his Diet Coke, he said, "Here's what's gonna happen; you will be reinstated into the United States Special Forces with the rank of captain. Also, as of noon today, you are relieved of all your desk duties as a Director of the Special Activities Division for the Central Intelligence Agency. You're going back as a Field Agent. For this operation, that is why you are going to be reinstated into the U.S. Army Special Operations Command. It's been a long briefing so go to lunch, then go home get your passport, and pack some of your stuff because, you're going back to our Special Training Facility in Quantico for a refresher in the Field Training Course, in our Special Training Facility known as the FARM. Your colleagues, Lieutenant Commander Carl, and Lieutenant Commander Chris are gonna go through the same refresher course, as you will be going through in Saudi Arabia."

After lunch, I took my briefcase, secured all my things on my desk, got into my Lamborghini Countach, and drove home. Exactly at noon, I took a shower and started to pack for my trip. However, the only thing that I packed was an extra pair of shorts, some sneakers, and some socks because I packed my sweatpants and everything else in my so-called duffel bag, which I always kept at the ready. When I graduated from the CIA Training Academy for the first time, I was always taught to keep a go bag while I was serving in the U.S. military.

It was 3:30 p.m. and my phone rang, I picked it up, and the voice on the other side of the phone, said, "Hello Mark it's me, Brian, I'm supposed to drive you to Andrew Air Force Base because you have a plane to catch to go to South Carolina." I recognized the voice. It was another friend that I knew from back in the day.

"I am ready for pickup now," I said. The car that pulled up was a black Chevy Suburban, and it did have United States government plates on it. I recognized Brian because we served in the same unit, in the special forces.

So I asked Brian, "Brian, what do you do nowadays since you retired from the military?"

"I work for the same agency as you do, except I'm in the Science and Tech Division," he said.

I laughed and said, "No way," so I asked him, "What happened to Kent and what have you been up to since he left the 101st Airborne Division?"

He said that he is still working for the company known as or formally known as Blackwater, now they are known as Academy. Brian had the same clarence as I did, so I said that's cool because, as far as I know, and the rumors I know, he might be coming with us on this mission. Me and Brian shared a few jokes, and when we arrived at the gate of Andrews Air Force Base, we flashed our CIA IDs, so we could get through the gate. When we got through the front gate, we boarded a Cessna 401 aircraft, for a three-hour flight, to South Carolina where the Central Intelligence Agency has its training and refresher courses facility.

After a three-hour flight, we landed at the CIA Training Facility. This facility was located on about 10 acres of land consisting of two training barracks, one airplane hangar, lots of training buildings, and three rifle and two pistol ranges.

As I was disembarking the aircraft that had flown me to the base, Col. Don came out of the airplane hangar and said, "Captain Mark."

"Yes, Sir."

"It is good to see you," he responded.

"You too, Sir." We shook hands, and we started to walk toward the airplane hangar.

Col. Don said, "Well, they finally granted you the rank of Captain Mr. Mark."

"Yes, Sir they sure did."

"What have you been doing with yourself for the last three years?"

"Well," I answered, "I have been sitting behind the desk in Langley and I was in charge of coordinating, all the anti-terrorism operations for the Central Intelligence Agency." Then I asked Captain Don the same question, "What have you been up to since Operation Iraqi Freedom when we got home?"

"Well, I still work for the U.S. government these days except nowadays I work for the company called Academy," he said, "Well okay Mark, let's go and I will take you to the supply room where you will pick up your camouflage fatigues, make sure that they are Woodland camouflage, and start report to barracks number two because starting tomorrow I just start working and kicking your behind."

We arrived at the Central Intelligence Agency's training facility at 4 p.m., and I picked up my Woodland camouflage gear and reported to barracks number two. There, I met one of my training officers and instructors, who I would be working with for the next five weeks. He knew me. My instructor's name was Robert, and he said, "Mr. Mark, I do not have a lot of time to fool around and I do not have time to pencil you through this. Drop your stuff over there next to the wall on the right side and you can take the lower bunk."

I said, "But Sir, there's nobody here. Am I going to be the only trainee in this particular refresher course?"

Instructor Robert looked at me and he asked, "What do you think?"

Instructor Robert I knew him very well because he was one of my first weapons instructors and hand-to-hand combat instructors when I was going through the selection process, for the special forces in Fort Bragg, South Carolina, when I enlisted in the U.S. Army Special Forces for the first time. So what I did was I put my duffel bag with my newly issued camouflage gear and fatigues next to the wall of my bunk and went right to sleep, and I did not wake up and tell, 6 a.m., the next morning.

At 6 a.m., a buzzer sounded and the voice on the intercom said, "Captain Mark, please report in full camouflage gear outside of your barracks in 15 minutes."

My instructor, Don, greeted me in front of the barracks and said, "You have five minutes to run to the Pistol Training Range."

This particular exercise was to test my physical condition. After a 10-minute run, I finally arrived at the pistol range. When I reported to the pistol range instructor Don and instructor Robert, who was in charge of my marksmanship refresher course, met me. At the range on the table on one of the stations there laid three types of weapons, number one was a 9 mm Glock 17, the second one was TT 76 2 x 25 pistol and the last one was a K 47 76 2 x 39 rifle with a folding stock laying on a table.

The instructor Robert said, "This particular exercise will check your marksmanship capability with these particular weapons."

My target was already hooked up on the target board downrange. Instructor Robert Kennedy at my station took the binoculars to his eyes and said, "Okay Captain Wrobel, load your weapon and show me what you can do."

I took the 9 mm Glock 17 and fired a few shots, and they all ended up in the center of the target. The same thing I managed to do with the TT 76 2 x 25 pistol and the same thing I achieved with my 76 2 x 39 AK-47s, what a folding stock rifle. So after I completed my weapons qualifications, the instructor said, "Not bad. You still shoot pretty darn good."

The next morning, another test came and this time, I had been tested on my ability and hand-to-hand combat training, which I passed with flying colors. Finally, Friday the next morning, I had to be tested and recertified for jumping out of an airplane with equipment. I passed that test with a grade of 100%. On Saturday night finally, I was ordered to report to the hangar of the airfield in which case I received my final briefing from Captain Don.

First Captain Don said, "Congratulations on completing your recertification and refresher course. Now I'm going to brief you on your mission and on the airplane that you'll be flying to get this mission accomplished. This particular aircraft is called King Air 90, however, this plane is also equipped with a computer system and software that will operate very sensitive surveillance equipment including VHF and HF radios and two radial missile jammers, and it also operates three high-definition photo and video cameras." Captain Don continued his presentation, "This aircraft is also equipped with four parachutes and this particular aircraft is also equipped with a self-destruct sequence where and when you push the button to activate it. Just before you guys leave the aircraft, the self-destruct sequence is to be activated in case you guys get yourself shut down, by the Israelis, under no circumstances this airplane and its equipment is to fall under any circumstances into the enemy's hands." Captain Don continued his brief, he said, "Mark here is another piece of equipment, that you will be issued with, it is a pen and yes it is capable of writing, however this particular pen when you push the top of the pen, it activates a sort of homing beacon. This particular beacon locator beacon to be exact is connected to a pager that a special recovery agent carries so that she knows that you guys have been shut down and so she can find you and guide you safely to our lines."

"Who is the recovery agent for this operation?"

"Her name is Maha. That is all I'm prepared to tell you."

"Excuse me, Captain," I said, "Maha's name sounds familiar. Is it the same Maha that used to have a YouTube channel?"

"I cannot confirm or deny this particular question, and Captain Mark, don't you be going and falling in love with one of those Arab women," Captain Don replied.

"Okay Sir," I said.

"No, no, you don't have to explain yourself to anybody who you fall in love with it's your business, however, what I have to tell you is for your own good because I want you to stay focused on the mission at this time. There is no Maha, there are no other girls that should be on your mind to stay focused on the mission and make sure that you all guys come home and bring back some good, actionable intelligence," said Captain Don.

"Captain Don, can I have a look at this file on our recovery, Agent Maha, if it's okay?"

Captain Don looked at me and said, "Sure, but you're only allowed to read the file."

"My eyes only?"

"In this case, yes," Captain Don answered.

I looked at the file in the airplane hangar where Captain Don has his office, I opened the file, and I saw the picture of Maha, I said, "Captain Don, that is that Palestinian girl, who used to have, a cool YouTube channel." As I read on, the file said that since the year 2009, she's been working as a medium personality on the Al Jazeera Network, and she works for Palestinian TV and Hamas TV as a news reporter. I said to Captain Don, "Well, I guess Maha got tired of being a YouTube babe and finally got herself a real job."

It was getting around 5 o'clock. "All Mark, I almost forgot, we issued you an emergency locator pan. However, there is one other piece of kit that I will have to issue to you right now, and that is, a poison pill with cyanide." Captain Don got into his desk drawer and said, "Look, Mark, all of you crewmembers will be issued with this type of pill. In case you guys get captured, we don't want you to spill the beans and lead vital information to the Israelites, you know. I know that if you or any of you guys get captured, you know that those Israelites will torture you guys for information."

I told Captain Don, "I will not need the suicide pill."

"I don't care if you need it or don't need it, if you are captured by the Israelites then you and your friends, can be tortured for information and we, as the United States cannot afford for you to let you and your friends bleed information to them," he said.

I asked Captain Don, "What are our chances for this mission to be successful?"

"Well, this mission I hate to tell you, Captain Mark, has about a 0.1% chance of success. However, the information that you guys can bring back from this operation can be very valuable to the future of the relationship between the United States, and the Arab world in general."

After the briefing, I went to my barracks, took off my combat boots, and took a little nap. At 6 p.m. I went to the chow hall to get some dinner. As the date of May 14, 2018, approached, there was more hustle and bustle on the training facilities, tarmac, and around the facility in general.

The next morning I was called into Captain Don's briefing again, he said, "Okay Mark let's go through this operation one more time, you will be flying on a commercial jet to King Hussein Aziz airbase in Saudi Arabia, in case you guys, get shut down when you guys parachute to safety, do not cluster together, split up, especially you Captain Mark, that is because there are only two people who have valuable information that might be valuable to the Israelites you and Captain Ken, Lieut. Carl and Lieut. Chris is flying the plane; they are only taxi drivers, that's all. If they get captured, it is not a big loss. Captain Mark, you may not like this, but you know, and I know, that this is the nature of the intelligence business. Here's how the mission will play out. You will fly out to Saudi Arabia on April 30th. That evening you will report to Col. John of the joint Saudi and American airbase intelligence command, and from there you will proceed on your flight to Israel on May 14th at night. Then you will linger at the station for three hours and record the conversation, between the President of the United States and the Prime Minister of Israel, if everything goes according to plan you should be back this time in Jordan and then the next morning all three of you will be on a plane in Jordan and then you'll be coming back home to Andrews Air Force Base for the debriefing if anything goes wrong you guys and your recovery agent Maha you will have to get back to Jordan on your own. In this case, because of the sensitivity of this mission, the United States has total and unequivocal deniability. What that means to you, Captain Mark, is that if you get into any trouble, the United States government will not come to your rescue. That is why in this case, I will ask you again and make you sign a waiver that you understand the terms and objectives of this mission."

After reading the non-disclosure agreement, I finally signed the papers, and the mission was about to get underway. Captain Don handed me my passport under a different name, which was Mohammed Aziz, and I was going on a pilgrimage to Mecca. However, this was my cover story. Captain Don also handed me a money belt which was filled with $100,000 in cash. I was also issued my cyanide pill and a pen with the emergency locator beacon.

Captain Don, with a big smile, said, "Your training here is complete. However, now the most important mission of your life is about to begin. This mission may open the door if it is successful. It may open the door for better living relations between us and the Arab world. Captain Mark, you better take this mission seriously because the success of this mission in reality depends on you. That's right, it all depends on you and your friends. Captain Mark, go ahead and get some sleep because you have a very hard day ahead. We are flying from our North Carolina training base to Anderson Air Force Base where you will board, a Saudi air passenger jet with your passport under the name of Mohammed Aziz and you will fly to Prince Bin Talal joint Saudi and American airbase. You are dismissed.

CHAPTER 2

Flight of R521

After a 10-hour flight from Andrews Air Force Base to Prince Faisal Airport in Saudi Arabia, where I flew on a commercial Saudi air aircraft. When I got off the airplane, I proceeded to go through Saudi immigration with my passport in hand. I approached one of the Saudi immigration checkpoints and placed my passport on the desk.

The immigration officer checked my passport and asked, "Is this your first visit to Saudi Arabia?"

"I traveled to Saudi Arabia on an American passport, but under a different name. In my passport, my name was Mohammed Aziz."

The Saudi immigration officer looked at me and asked, "Is your name Mohammed Aziz like it says in your passport?"

I said in Arabic, "Yes it is."

Then he asked, "Also is this your first time visiting Saudi Arabia?"

I answered, "In Arabic, yes, it is because I'm here on a pilgrimage to Mecca and Medina."

After all that, he stamped a Visa on my passport and said, "Enjoy your stay in Saudi Arabia." After I made my way from the Saudi immigration checkpoint. I saw that John was waiting there for me.

John came up to me, shook my hand, and said, "Mark, I see that you finally made the rank of captain."

I said to John, "Yes I did. What are you doing here? The last time I saw you, you were working for Carl's dad at the funeral home."

"Well, it's been a couple of years and now I work as a defense attaché in the U.S. Embassy here in Saudi Arabia because our dear United States

Air Force was nice enough to assign me to this job." John grabbed my bags, we walked outside of the airport, and we got into the Cadillac Escalade SUV.

John asked me, "So, Mark, do you want to sit up front or want to sit in the back?"

I told him to put my duffel bag in the back and let me sit up front. So we drove for an hour. I looked out of the window of the bulletproof SUV, and I saw Saudi Arabia's landscape. It was like driving through a future city. I thought I was in a Star Wars movie because the buildings and the hotels were very futuristic-looking.

After an hour's drive, we arrived at the Prince Bin Tala Joint Airbase. On the airplane hangar, the sign said, "AMERICAN JOINT SPECIAL OPERATIONS COMMAND."

As I was getting out of the SUV, a commanding officer of the base came out and he said, "Good morning, I trust you had a good flight."

I said, "The flight was not too bad, Sir."

The commanding officer's name was Walter. I knew him from Fort Bragg. He used to teach a course in radio communications as a special forces officer. I was part of his radio communications class.

As I walked into the airplane hangar, I recognized two of my friends, Lieutenant Carl and Lieutenant Chris. Captain Ken was coming out of the meteorological office and he handed me a folder with the latest weather reports to give to Col. Walt.

"Here are the weather reports that you requested Sir, Col. Walt."

After we had some coffee and donuts, Col. Walt said, "Please take your seat gentlemen because there are going to be some changes to your escape and flight plan. Here are some of the changes in case you get shut down. The strategy is if you have to bail out, there is another country where you can escape and that is the United Arab Emirates. It is called the country of Bahrain to be more specific. The U.S. Navy will have an E3 Orion Aircraft on station to monitor your mission. Good luck gentlemen, that's all for now.

So if everything is running on schedule you will depart Saudi Arabia tomorrow May 13th at midnight. You will fly low until you reach the city of Jerusalem, then the aircraft will climb to 150 feet. However, at that time, your recording and video cameras should be turned on. You stay at the station for three hours. Then hopefully if you guys are all in one piece, you haul ass to Jordan and land at King Hussein's joint American Special Forces Base. Or you fly as fast as you can to the country of Dubai and land in the Kings on Maktoum Royal Air Force Base. Now I suggest you guys, go over this plan again, because tomorrow is the 13th. You will still have all day here in Saudi Arabia until 11:30 p.m. At that time we will do all your pre-flight; then at midnight, your mission will kick off. Your plane has to be on the runway for five minutes before midnight. Is that understood, Lieutenant Carl? Is that understood, Lieutenant Chris?"

Chris and Carl answered in unison, "Yes Sir."

"It's 6:30 p.m. now, and today is May 13th so in this case, until tomorrow you guys are free to do whatever you want on this air base but tomorrow, you have to be back here in the hangar at 8:00 p.m.," Col. Walt said.

It was April 13th at midnight and Lieut. Commander Carl, Lieut. Commander Chris and I reported to the top-secret hangar at the Kings Bin Talal, Saudi Air Force Base. It was 8:00 p.m.

Col. Walter said, "Okay boys, let me check to make sure that we have attendance, Captain Mark," I said. "Present."

"Captain Ken." He answered, "Present."

"Lieutenant Commander Carl." "Present," he said.

"Lieutenant Commander Chris." "Present." He sent Col. Water to continue with the briefing.

"Gentleman today is the day that at midnight Operation Wrath of Saladin will kick off. All of your weapons and other gear are in front of you. However, in this case, you will have to remove all your American patches with the American flags and those will be replaced with the Russian flag. Your King Aircraft markings also will be replaced with the Russian flag as well. The reason for this is the Central Intelligence Agency has total deniability," he said.

Our team, which included Captain Mark and Captain Ken as Electronic Warfare Specialists, Lieutenant Commander Carl, and Lieutenant Commander Chris, changed into our flight suits. We removed the American flag patches from the flight suits and replaced them with the Russian ones.

Col. Walter said, "OK guys, let's take a seat, and let's go through the plan one more time. At midnight aircraft the King Air 90 takes off from the Prince Bin Talal Saudi Air Base, and after about an hour, you will be in Israeli airspace. The plane will climb to 18,000 feet. In this case, you boys will be on oxygen. However, before you reach the Israeli airspace, you make sure you have all of your surveillance equipment turned on and running. Yeah, we'll hang around in Israeli airspace for about 2-3 hours. Remember the President of the United States and the Prime Minister of Israel? We'll be meeting for three to four hours. At that time, it is your responsibility Lieutenant Commander Carl and Lieutenant Commander Chris to stay on station as long as possible. This will be up to you, Lieutenant Commander Carl, and Lieutenant Commander Chris. Now let's go over, the escape plan in case this whole plan goes south. First, put on your parachutes. The last person to leave the aircraft, his responsibility, is to hit the self-destruct button. When you jump out of the aircraft, do it together, however when you hit the ground, you will have to split up. Do not walk together in a desert; one person goes in one direction, and the other goes in the other direction. This is done in case you get captured by the Israelis. You do not leak classified information, that is because none of you know everything, so in case of capture, it will be difficult for them to put the pieces together of this operation. There are two escapes: one is the country of Jordan. The next country of escape is the United Arab Emirates United Arab Emirates. More specifically, the country is called Amana Bahrain."

The time is 11:45 p.m., and Captain Mark, Lieutenant Commander Carl, Lieutenant Commander Chris, and Captain Ken boarded the modified King Air aircraft. We put on our seat belts and we're prepared for takeoff.

Lieutenant Commander Carl talked to the control tower, "Saudi Tower, this is Flight R521. Request permission to taxi the control tower."

"This is the Saudi Tower Flight R521. Please take runway 212, right."

Lieutenant Commander Carl said, "Saudi Tower, this is Flight R521 at runway 212 right request permission for takeoff."

Saudi Arabia responded, "Roger Flight R521 you have when coming from the east about 5 miles an hour. You're clear for takeoff, Saudi Tower, out."

As we flew into the night, Lieutenant Commander Chris said, "Hello Mark, it's nice to see you. I thought that you retired from the agency by now."

"I could say the same thing about you."

"I thought that you were living in the Bahamas, Mark," Chris said.

"No such luck."

"So Chris," I said, "What made you take a mission like this?"

"Hey Mark, you really want to know the truth. I would rather fly missions like this with you guys than argue with that barracuda of mine," he said.

As we were flying, we were getting closer and closer to the Israeli Airspace.

We were getting closer to our target and Lieutenant Commander Carl said, "Lieut. Commander Chris, Captain Mark, stop your conversations."

Captain Ken said, "Okay Mark, let's start our music."

We turned on our surveillance cameras and our recording devices, the VHF and HF radios. The time was 10 a.m. and the President of the United States and the Prime Minister of Israel were in the building called the Knesset and they were in his office. As we were flying closer and closer to the territory of Israel, to be more exact closer to the territory of Jerusalem, suddenly, a missile warning alarm started to go off.

Commander Carl said, "Chris, take invasive action."

I said, "Captain Ken, I'm tracking a missile launch on my scope."

"I didn't know that those heaps had missiles that accurate and that close to their cities. That is one of the reasons we are here to tell the Americans the bad news," Captain Ken said.

I said, "I've got another missile on my scope, Lieutenant Commander call to take evasive action." Suddenly, we felt and heard a big bang and a thump.

Lieutenant Commander Chris said, "Boys, we lost one of our engines."

I said, "Guys, let's get the hell out of here! Let's head for the Negev desert." Suddenly, another missile warning sounded.

I said, "Here it comes another missile!"

Meanwhile, our surveillance equipment kept recording what was going on around us. In the Parliament Building, another missile warning sounded.

I said, "Looks like those heaps launched another missile." We heard another thump and a bang.

Lieutenant Commander Chris said, "Boys, we lost another engine. Begin emergency evacuation procedures."

Lieutenant Commander Carl shouted, "Boys, strap on your parachutes. We are going down!"

Lieutenant Commander Chris, in this case, the copilot said, "Mayday, Mayday, Mayday this is Flight R521. We are going down northeast of Jerusalem!"

As we reached the edge of the Negev desert, Lieutenant Commander Carl gave the order to Lieutenant Commander Chris to open the door.

"Alright boys," Carl yelled, "prepare to jump!"

We jumped out of the airplane; we floated in the air for 30 seconds, and then we felt a jolt and the parachute opened. After the parachute opened, we floated down to the ground in the middle of the Negev desert. Captain Ken landed first, I landed right behind him, and Lieutenant Commander Carl and the tenant Commander Chris landed last. The desert heat was very hot, we were very angry.

Captain Ken was really mad. He said, "Look guys, these Fuckin' Hebes set us up! How did those stupid heaps know that we were flying over their airspace?"

Lieutenant Commander Chris yelled, "I bet you I know, some Fuck wanted us to get burned!"

"It doesn't matter who set up this mission to fail or to end up like this, but the most important thing is for us to get home alive. We better start moving because the sun is coming up soon and it's gonna get hot in this desert pretty soon. We should have two to three hours of an easy march. I understand that there are bodies at the Central Intelligence Agency who told us that in case of mission failure and if we do land on the ground, we have to split up, but I say if they screwed us like this then the heck with their instructions. Alright, guys, we're gonna have to start walking north and we will go to the Jordanian border because it is the closest thing where we can get help. It's about 30 miles from here. It's not too bad. About 10 miles into the march, we will activate our emergency locator pens that we were issued, but not until then. Captain Ken, you will be the person to lead this march. Lieutenant Commander Chris, we'll follow him and then Captain Mark, you will go behind Lieutenant Commander Chris and bring up the rear; everyone keep up," said Lieutenant Commander Carl.

CHAPTER 3

Into the Desert Sand

After landing in the middle of the desert I said, "Okay gentlemen, here is the situation. We all know that we were probably set up, and this mission was set up to fail in the first place. However, this is not what is important at this point, the important part is to get back to our line, and if we do that will be okay. One thing is for sure, is that, that those Yates will definitely try to put us in prison if we don't start moving in the next couple of minutes. Gentlemen I said before we start moving, let's check our equipment and weapons."

Lieutenant Commander Carl said, "I got five magazines for my AK-47 Su." I said I had the same.

Lieutenant Commander the commander Chris said, "I've got the same." I said I had the same amount for my AK-47 Su.

Captain Ken said, "Let's check our pistol ammunition that we all have for magazines and our TT 33 pistols."

Lieutenant Commander Carl said, "Check for magazines."

Captain Mark said, "I had the same."

Lieutenant Commander Chris said, "I got the same."

After we checked our weapons, I said, "Gentlemen, let's start moving because we will have an hour or two of easy march, before the sun gets really hot."

Meanwhile, back in Jerusalem, the Prime Minister of Israel gets a telephone call from one of his antiaircraft missile battery commanders yelling.

Benghazi told the Prime Minister, "Mr. Prime Minister, we have shut down an American spy aircraft."

The Israeli Prime Minister was shocked. He said, "Do we know who sent the aircraft?"

Commander Yanni Benghazi, told the Prime Minister, "The markings on the plane are of Russian origin."

The Israeli Prime Minister said, "Please put me in touch with the Israeli Ministry of Defense."

The Israeli Prime Minister's secretary said, "The Israeli Defense Minister by the name John Feinberg is on the other line, Mr. Prime Minister."

"Hello John, this is Yanni, the Prime Minister of Israel. Did you guys hear about the spy plane being shut down in the Israeli airspace?"

"Yes Sir, there are two types of brigades, three armored cars, and two helicopters trying to catch the spies and from what the Mossad Intelligence can analyze from the wreck, the plane was sent by Americans to spy on us."

The Israeli Prime Minister said, "John, I want these American spies brought in as soon as possible because I do want to find out what they are up to."

The Defense Minister John Feinberg said, "Yes Mr. Prime Minister, we have been put on alert, our borders police, and we are putting together a division of tanks and armored cars, and two helicopters to search for those American spies."

Meanwhile, Lieutenant Commander Chris, Lieutenant Commander Carl, Captain Ken, and I were tracking through the desert trying to reach the border of Jordan. We walked for a couple of hours; the sun was getting intensively hot.

I said, "OK guys, let's take a break, Captain Ken. Let's check on map coordinates to make sure that we are on the right track to the Jordanian border." We checked the coordinates on the map and we were on the right track.

As we were getting up to continue our march towards the Jordanian border, I said, "Everyone stay down."

I put the edge of my survival knife up in the prone position, put my ear to the desert floor, and listened for a couple of minutes, what I heard was the clicking of the tracks of the Israeli tanks, and a few minutes later we heard and saw two Apache Israeli gunships helicopters.

Captain Ken yells, "Everyone hide behind the sand dunes!"

Lieutenant Commander Carl and Lieutenant Commander Chris hid behind the same sand dune. As we heard the rotors of the Apache gunship helicopters, we said to ourselves, *"Holy cow, those Yates really got us."*

Lieutenant Commander Chris and Lieutenant Commander Carl asked me, "What are your orders, Captain Mark? Does the previous order still stand, that me and Lieutenant Commander Chris and Captain Ken, cover your escape or do we stand and fight?"

"Lieutenant Commander Carl, we are not going to take on the entire Israeli army. We only got five magazines for our weapons and that includes four Ak47 SU. So here are your orders and choices. We can all end up in the Israeli prison, or one of us can make it out of here and tell the whole world what happened here and maybe someone will get you guys out of the hellhole. That the Israeli prison is..."

Suddenly, we heard a voice that spoke broken English, with a European accent, "You people are surrounded. There is no escape for you." That was true.

Lieutenant Commander Carl and Lieutenant Commander Chris said, "Listen up guys, we will have to provide an escape for Captain Mark here. That is because if we end up in the Israeli prison, it may not be so bad for us. However, you Mark might have a problem because you have too much knowledge of American national security."

So I said, "Here is what we're going to do; I will fire first and then I will run like hell, trying to make it to the Jordanian border. You guys will provide cover fire for me."

"May I say, gentlemen, that this plan sucks."

"Yes, Captain Mark, we all know that this plan sucks, but somebody has got to make it out alive and tell the people what happened here," Lieut. Cmdr. Chris said, "Plus, somebody has to speak on our behalf in Washington, D.C., and try to get a fair case. The honor is yours, Mark."

"Listen guys, this type of honor I don't even want."

"We don't care if you want this honor or not, however, you are stuck with it," Lieutenant Commander Carl, Lieutenant Commander Chris, and Captain Ken said in unison.

"Okay guys, here's what I have in mind," Captain Ken said, "here's the plan, Carl and Chris. We will try to hold them off as long as possible."

"But Sir, that is a good idea. However, you know what Israeli prisons are like," I said.

"We already spoke about that, Captain Mark," he said.

"Okay Sir," Captain Ken said.

"Yes Sir," said Lieutenant Commander Carl.

"Yes Sir," said Lieutenant Commander Chris.

"On my mark, gentlemen begin firing," Captain Ken said, "Run Mark."

So when my crew began firing on the Israelis, and I started to run everything, turned into a major disaster. As I looked back, I saw Lieutenant Commander Chris and all of my crew being taken away, tied up, put on trucks, and driven away into the Desert of Bud Shaba. As I was running, I saw a little Jordanian bird's helicopter, H60 firing rockets and two machine guns so that I could get away. A couple of miles when I got away from the shoot-out, one of the little birds landed. The Jordanian pilot waved to me and said, hurry up, get in. I got into the back of the h 60 little bird helicopter and then I just passed out. The next thing I remember, I woke up in the Jordanian Military Hospital.

They said, "Captain Mark, I am Lieut. Col. Dr. Aziz. In a few days, you will be going home."

"Dr. Aziz, does anyone know what happened to my crew?" I asked.

"Well, in this case, unfortunately, I got some bad news. Your crew was taken prisoner by the Israelis."

"All of them?" I asked.

Dr. Aziz said, "Unfortunately, yes, in this case, but fortunately, do not concern yourself with that. We have to make sure you're well enough to go home."

A few days later, I was on my way home on the diplomatic Air Force 2 that was provided by the U.S. State Department, and after 10 hours of flight, we landed at Andrews Air Force Base in Washington, D.C.

CHAPTER 4

Heroes Homecoming

After spending three months in the Jordanian Military Base and after 30 debriefings, I was able to finally go home back to the U.S. After an eight-hour flight onboard the Delta Airlines plane; I landed at Ronald Reagan Airport, in Washington, D.C., where my friend Frank met me at the gate.

"Hey Mark," Frank said, "how was your trip?"

"The trip itself was not so bad, but what happened to my team is," I said, "Hey Frank, do me a favor, don't tell my boss Mike that I am back in town yet."

When we were driving from the airport, I saw a sign for Motel 6. I went into the lobby and checked in. I told the clerk that I would like to rent a room for one week, and he said okay. I checked into the room and went right to sleep.

The next morning, I called Amber, Lieutenant Commander Carl's wife, "Hello Amber. I guess you heard what happened to Carl."

"When are you coming home, Mark?" Amber asked.

"Listen, Amber, to answer your question. I'm not sure, that is because I'm gonna hang around Washington, D.C., to see what went wrong. I'm going to find out who actually set up this mission to fail," I said.

"I could get on an Amtrak train here in Wilmington, Delaware, and be with you in Washington, D.C., in three hours," Amber said.

I said, "Amber, this is some serious business. Somebody set us up and set up the mission to fail and believe me, I'm gonna find out what is really going on here. However, it is better in this case for you not to show up, but you're going to do whatever you want to do. So as you are coming to Washington, D.C., you gonna do what I tell you to do and move how I tell you to because this mission really stinks. So I'm just going to warn you, this is not a joke; if you gonna come down to Washington, be aware of these things," I asked Amber, "how is Carla taking this?"

"Well," Amber said, "she wants to buy a train ticket also to D.C., and she wants to find out what's going on."

"Amber, it's better for you not to come to Washington, at this point. However, Carla would be better for this job, so tell her to give me a call in this hotel room. The phone number is 206–321–6211. Tell Carla to give me a call and I will meet her in Washington, D.C.'s Grand Central Station. Okay, Amber, I will talk to you later." Meanwhile, back in Delaware, Carla was talking to Amber.

"Carla Mark is back," Amber said

"Where is he?"

Amber told Carla, "Mark is staying in Washington, D.C., for a while."

"Well, guess what?" Carla said to Amber, "he is not staying there by himself. I'm going to join him in Washington; what is his phone number?" Carla asked Amber.

"Mark's phone number is 206-321-6211. Mark is staying at Motel 6, a couple blocks down from the Capitol building," replied Amber.

As I got back to my motel room, as I was about to open the door and walk in, my phone in my motel room began to ring. I answered the phone and on the other side of the phone; I heard a familiar voice. It said, "Hello Mark, it's me, Carla."

"Hi Carla, I guess you heard what happened to my team, and that includes your brother, Carl," I said.

"Yes, I know," Carla said.

"Carla, I have to tell you something," I said, "what happened to Carl should have never happened." Carla got a little mad at me.

"Why didn't you protect my brother?"

"Look Carla, when it comes to your brother, he always protected me. Even on this operation, he protected me, in this case as well, but don't you worry, we will deal with it. We will both find out who or what is behind the failure of this operation. I will, with your help get your brother back and my friend as well," I said.

"Okay Mark, I am taking the train tomorrow at 9 a.m. from Wilmington, Delaware Amtrak station. I will arrive in Washington, D.C., tomorrow at noon."

"Okay Carla, I will see you tomorrow at noon at the Washington, D.C. Grand Central Station," I said, then hung up. Then I went right to sleep in my Motel 6 room.

At 5:30 a.m., my phone rang in my motel room. I picked up the phone, and on the other side of the receiver was a familiar voice that said, "Hello Mark, I have some information, that might be of some interest to you regarding the failure of Operation Wrath of Saladin, and the abduction of your crew."

The voice on the other side of the line did sound familiar. I asked, "Is this you, Joe?"

"Yes, it's me," he said.

"Mark, if you want this information, I can meet you. I can meet you at the Richard Nixon Bar and Grill on Columbus Avenue at 4:30 p.m. this afternoon."

I got in the shower and got myself dressed, and then I went downstairs to talk to the receptionist at the front desk, a nice lady. She was about 35 years old. She had dark hair and dark eyes; she was originally from Cuba. I asked her if I could rent an extra room on the same floor, and the lady whose name was Esmeralda, said that this would be okay. The check to pay for the room is $500. I told the lady that I needed that extra room for a friend of mine who was coming to visit.

It was 11:55 a.m. I paid the lady for the room and then I called a taxi. The taxicab arrived in 15 minutes. I told the driver, "Grand Central Station, please."

The traffic was kind of heavy as it usually is in Washington, D.C., this time in the morning. The trip to the train station took me 20 minutes. As I got into the building and saw Carla was waiting for me already.

I said, "Hello Carla, it is good to see you."

"Mark, what are we going to do about bringing Carl and your flight crew back home?" she asked.

"Do not worry Carla, because in about an hour, I'm meeting with a guy at a restaurant, Richard Nixon's Bar and Grill," I said.

I whistled for the taxicab, told the driver Milwaukee Avenue; was where the Motel 6 was located, and told the driver to wait for us. So Carla and I checked into the motel. Carla dropped off her luggage and we went back to the taxicab.

Carla asked, "Why are we in such a hurry?"

I said, "Because in 15 minutes we're going to meet a guy at the Richard Nixon Bar and Grill Restaurant that might have some information about what's happening to Carl and my crew."

We arrived at the restaurant, Carla and I walked into the bar and ordered two Martinis one for me and the other one for Carla. As we were sitting down and drinking, Martinis, a good friend of mine, Joe C. walked into the bar.

"Hi Mark, I heard what happened to you guys," he said.

Carla asked Joe, "What is really going on here? What is really happening to Carl and the rest of his flight crew?"

"Mark and Carla, let's grab a seat at a private booth in the restaurant part of the bar."

"So who is this Joe C.?" Carla asked.

"Joe C. is a friend who used to work with me in the information technology division CIA before I transferred to the special activities division of the CIA," I said.

So as Joe, Carla, and I sat down in the booth, Joe pulled out a very interesting folder. Carla and Joe looked at the content of the folder.

Joe said, "Mark and Carla, look at this."

The folder there was a top-secret, Delta-level protocol. It read that Delta-level top-secret clearance required the flight crew of R521 to be exchanged for the two Israeli soldiers who were kidnapped by the PLO. The American Flight crew was to be used as a bargaining chip in the negotiations between the PLO and the Israeli government. After the negotiations are over Israeli government may do whatever it sees fit with the flight crew.

After Carla and I finished reading the attached top-secret protocol, Carla asked Joe in a very angry, tone of voice, "You sent Mark and his crew to be used as a football in the negotiation between the Israelis and the

Palestinians!"

Joe said, "Look, Carla, I know that you are upset right now, but you should know that people like Mark, Carl, and his friends know what kind of job they get themselves into. Mark and your brother, Carl, took the oath to the United States Constitution, and believe me, Carla, people like Mark and your brother are the toughest people on this earth, and our country needs men like them to keep us safe."

The time was 10 p.m., and the Richard Nixon Bar was giving the customers a last call. Therefore, Joe, Carla, and I left the bar.

"Listen, Carla," I said, "we're not going to be able to do anything else tonight, so let's go back to the motel. Let's pick up where we left off tomorrow."

It was 7:30 the next morning. Carla called Amber, and Amber asked Carla, "How are things going there in D.C.?"

"Not too good, Mark and his flight crew are in deep trouble," Carla answers, "from the information that I know, did you know that Mark and his flight crew were to be used, as a political football in the negotiation between, the Israelis and the Palestinian?"

"Listen, Mark is in trouble, yes but Mark knows what he's doing."

Amber said, "I am coming to you guys in the morning to D.C. I'm going to call Mark and tell him I'm coming."

After an hour, I got a phone call, and on the other side of the phone was Amber. She said, "I'm coming to Washington, D.C., to help you guys out."

"Amber, you going to do what?!" I yelled.

Amber said, "I'm going to come to Washington, D.C., to be there if you guys need me."

"Okay Amber," I said, "You can come because I know that if I tell you not to come here, you're going to come here anyway because you are stubborn. That is okay because if I know what we are planning to do, I'm going to need all of your stubbornness and then some."

Amber said, "Okay Mark, I'm going to be arriving at the Washington, D.C., Grand Central Station tomorrow on the noon train. Also, I'm going to pay a taxicab so you don't have to pick me up from the train station."

"Okay, Amber, I will see you here at 1:30 tomorrow afternoon," I said.

After I finished the conversation with Amber, I hung up the phone and started to make phone calls again. I called my friend Jack, in the Arabic language department in Langley, and I asked him, "Hey Jack, can you send me a few things, like the Arabic learning CD from topics entertainment, English and Arabic dictionary, and the Arabic living language audio CDs?"

"Why do you need all these things?" Jack asked me.

"Jack, in this case, you will have to hear about it on the news in a couple of weeks," I said.

Jack said, "Okay, Mark, where do you want these things sent?"

I said, "Send them to the Columbus Avenue Post Office at 321 Columbus Ave., Washington, D.C., P.O. Box 221."

"Mark, can I be more helpful?" Jack asked.

"No Jack, not at this time. If my boss Mike knew that I was back in the world, he would have my behind in the ringer, so this does not go beyond this conversation."

He said, "Okay Mark, you should receive the package with the things that you requested in 24 hours in your P.O. Box."

"Thank you, Jack. I appreciate everything you've done," I said.

"Anytime, Mark, that's what friends are for," he replied. After I finished my conversation on the phone, it was after midnight, and I went back to sleep.

The next morning I woke up at 7:30 a.m., I knew that today Amber was coming to Washington, D.C., to help us; me and Carla, I mean. It was around 8 a.m., Carla and I walked down to the motel lobby and whistled for a taxi. We got into the taxi and said, "Columbus Avenue Post Office, please." We got there in 15 minutes, and she and I went inside the post office. I got a key, and I got into my P.O. Box. I got the things that my friend Jack sent me.

"Hey Mark, why do you need all the Arabic learning things like the Arabic dictionary and the Arabic learning CDs?" Carla asked.

I answered, "They're not for me, they are for Amber."

Then Carla asked, "You're telling me that Amber is coming here to D.C.?"

"Yes she is," I said.

Carla said but my question to you is, "What can she help us with in this situation? She does not speak good Arabic."

"Carla, I know. That is why she is going to get a crash course in the Arabic language."

Carla said, "This is not good."

I said, "Look Carla I don't want her here either, but you know how stubborn she is, once she sets her mind on something there's no way to talk her out of it, and let me tell you something that is, a very good thing about her."

"So who is this Amber, you may ask?"

"Amber is my best friend's wife. She has a very sparkling personality, and she's very stubborn."

"Okay, Mark Amber's coming on this mission," Carla said.

"Okay, Carla, but she better follow our every order and she better do what we tell her to do, or this mission will end up in the crapper like the other one did," I said.

It was getting closer to noon. I said, "Carla, let's go to a motel lobby and whistle for a taxicab. Let's go pick up Amber at the Washington, D.C., Grand Central Station."

So me and Carla walked down to the Motel 6 lobby and whistled taxicab.

I told the driver to "Grand Central Train Station please."

So we arrived at the Grand Central Station just as Amber was walking through the lobby to the exit door.

I said, "Hello Amber, it is good to see you after all."

As Carla, Amber, and I walked to the taxi stand, my cell phone rang, and on the other side was Joe C.

"Hello Joe, what's going on?" I asked.

"I need to meet you and Carla at the Richard Nixon Bar and Grill Restaurant in an hour," Joe said.

I asked Joe, "What's going on?"

"The situation has gotten a little bit more complicated."

"Okay, Joe, I will see you in an hour."

Carla, Amber, and I got into the taxicab, and we said, "Motel 6 Columbus Avenue, please."

As we got out of the taxicab, I went into my room and Carla went to hers. Carla's room had a second bed. I went into my room and changed into one of my other dress-up suits. I walked out of my room and I knocked on the door of Amber's and Carla's room.

Carla opened the door and Amber asked, "Mark, can I go with you guys to the Richard Nixon Bar and Grill Restaurant?"

I said, "No Amber, that is because I have a more important job to do here. You're going to stay here in this room and you going to learn the Arabic language and I need you to learn it fast." I handed Amber the envelope with the Arabic learning material that I had received earlier from my friend, Jack.

"Okay, Amber, get learning and fast. Carla and I will be back in two hours by that time, I want you to have mastered all the basic phrases in Arabic," I said.

So, in this case, Carla and I walked to the Motel 6 lobby and whistled for a taxicab, and I said, "Richard Nixon Bar and Restaurant, please." We arrived at the restaurant in 20 minutes. Joe C. was already there waiting for us.

Joe asked, "Mark and Carla, can I get you guys something to drink?"

I said, "A glass of Coke will do."

Carla said, "I will have the same."

"So what is this hot information that you have that we have had to get here in a hurry?" I asked Joe.

"Well," Joe said as he pulled out a folder, "the government has held a trial and they have sentenced the whole flight crew for spying on life imprisonment and hard labor, this particular sentence will go into effect in 90 days."

Carla said, "Mark, we don't have a lot of time to pencil through this."

I said, "Yes we got to act fast."

I said, okay Carla, let's go. I have a lot of phone calls I have to make.

Carla and I got back into the taxicab and we got back to the motel.

When we got back to the rooms, I asked Amber, "How is your Arabic lesson going?"

I gave Amber an Arabic word quiz. I wanted to see how much Arabic vocabulary she had learned. I was surprised at Amber's progress in learning the Arabic language.

I said, "Well, Amber, your Arabic language is getting better. Listen, Carla, stay here with Amber and help her with her Arabic language because I have some phone calls that I have to make." So I went back to my room, and I started to make phone calls.

The first person I called was my friend Fred, who used to work for the Department of Documents in the CIA. He retired two years after I entered the military and the CIA service. He was one of my lead instructors as I was going through the CIA spy school officially known as the Farm. So I called my friend Fred. I dialed my friend's number and his phone rang and Fred answered.

I said, "Fred, I need to see you ASAP."

He said, "I know what happened to your team."

It was around 1:30 p.m., in the afternoon, I was sitting in my hotel room, and I made one more phone call. I knew that I had better do this in a hurry because Amber, Carla, and I were supposed to meet with Fred the forger at the Richard Nixon Bar and Restaurant. The phone call that I made was to my friend Eric. So who is Eric you might be asking? Eric was a good friend of mine when I started to work for the Central Intelligence Agency. So I called up my friend Eric.

"Hello Eric, it's your friend, Mark. What are you up to?" I asked him.

"Nothing much, Mark," he said, "I heard what happened to you guys. Why don't you bring yourself and your friends over here?"

"Where is that?" I asked.

"United Arab Emirates, the country of Bahrain, to be exact. Why don't you and your friends come over here for vacation?" he asked.

I said, "Okay, Eric, I will see you there in a couple of days." When I finished talking to Eric, I hung up the phone. I knocked on the door of Carla and Amber's room.

I said, "Hurry up you girls, because we have to meet my friend Freddie at the Richard Nixon Bar and Restaurant in a couple of minutes."

Carla, Amber, and I walked down to the lobby of the motel and we whistled for a taxi. The taxi arrived, and I said, "Richard Nixon Bar and Restaurant, please." My friend Freddie was already waiting there for us.

"What's going on Freddie?" I asked.

"Would you guys like something to drink?" Freddie asked us.

I said, "I'll take a drink of Diet Coke, so what is so important that we had to see you?"

"I've got some information that is hot off the press. Now Mark and Carla, listen up. You to Amber. Mark's flight crew is about to be exchanged for a Palestinian prisoner named Anna Moon."

"You mean that girl who was part of the kidnapping plot of the Israeli soldier a couple of months back in the city of Nablus in the West Bank?" I asked.

"The bigger problem is if the Palestinians don't agree to this deal, the Israelis are using the flight crew as leverage and what the deal is if the Palestinians do not agree to deal with the flight crew is in deep trouble."

I asked Fred, "What else do you know that I don't know about this situation?"

"Not much but if this deal fails Israelis might do something horrible to the flight crew, but don't worry guys Joe C., through nonofficial channels, bought you months of time to clean up this situation."

"Alright Fred, I'm going to need three Muslim countries' passports: one Arabian, the other one Egyptian, and the other one has to be from the UAE," I said.

"My friend, I am away ahead of you, I got you three plane tickets for the United Arab Emirates, next week the only thing that we have to do is to get you your passports and you're right Mark those passports have to be Arab countries, but Mark don't worry about that because I brought all the equipment necessary, to make this happen," said Fred.

After we finished our drinks, we all got into the taxicab and went back to Motel 6, where we were staying. We walked into the room, and then Fred hung up a yellow background. That is because most passport photos in the Arab world require a yellow background for the passport photo. So in this case, my friend Fred took a picture of Amber under the yellow background. The second person who had to get her picture taken for her passport was Carla, and the last person was me.

Fred said, "Listen up. You guys, especially you Amber, and Carla, will have an uphill battle. Carla, not so much you, however, you Amber, will have a little bit of a hard time. That is because you don't speak that good of an Arabic language."

However, I said, "Amber, listen, no matter what happens, you're coming with us."

My friend Fred said, "Mark I will have your passports delivered to you in a couple of days, now listen Amber I said you will travel with us to the country of Bahrain and the United Arab Emirates. However you will not travel there under your real name of Amber, your new name will be Miriam Khalifa bin Laden."

"Why can I not travel with you guys to the UAE under my real name?" Amber asked me.

I said, "Amber, the reason that you're going to travel with us, under a different name is because we don't want to raise suspicion of any other intelligence services."

"But Mark is in the name, Bin Laden going to raise alarm bells?

"In one way you might be thinking right, however, you have to understand that the name Bin Laden still commands a major respect in the Arab world especially when your identity papers will say that you're a niece and an air to the Bin Laden Construction Company in Saudi Arabia. Even Israelis have some respect when it comes to the Bin Laden Construction Company."

We met my friend Fred on Wednesday. We chilled out for a little bit then went to the Richard Nixon Bar.

Friday finally arrived, and I said, "Amber, me and Carla are going to the post office to pick up some stuff. You're going to stay here, and I want you to start learning things about the Bin Laden Construction Company. You can use the materials that Fred left for you. Carla and I will be back in an hour."

So me and Carla went down to the lobby of Motel 6 and called for a taxicab. The taxicab arrived, and we got in. I said, "To the post office, please." We arrived at the post office, I went to my P.O. Box, opened the box, and found three passports. One for Amber under the name Miriam I. Khalifa Bin Laden, Amber's passport was from Saudi Arabia. Another passport arrived, which was Egyptian. Under the name Miriam Ismaili, this passport was for Carla.

While we were at the post office, a lady was sitting in a window as Carla was leaving said, "Excuse me, I have a package for the two of you."

The package came from the United Arab Emirates. It was my friend, Eric. We picked up all the things from the P.O. Box, and the package from the post office. I whistled for a taxi, Carla and I got in and I said, "To the Motel 6 on Columbus Avenue, please."

It took us 20 minutes to arrive at our Motel 6. Amber was already waiting there for us; it was 2:30 p.m. Carla and Amber went back to their rooms.

I said, "Wait just a minute, I have a package for Amber. I don't know but my friend Eric sent this note he said to you." So me and Amber went into the room, Amber opened up the package, and in that package was an Arab Abaya.

What is an Abaya you may ask?

The Abaya is an Islamic outfit that is worn by Muslim women in a country like Saudi Arabia.

The Abaya itself consists of two pieces. One piece is a long black dress, and the other piece is the veil that covers the face where you can only see the woman's eyes.

Amber said, "Mark, I am not going to wear that."

"Amber yes you are, that is because where we are going as a White European woman with blonde hair and blue eyes, you're going to stick out like a sore thumb," I said, "okay Carla you are going to work with Amber, you're going to teach her how to walk in these Muslim clothes.

Amber thought about it a little bit and she said, "Okay, Mark."

Meanwhile, I went back to my room to make one more phone call to my friend Eric. I called Eric, and Eric answered the phone.

I said, "Hello Eric, it is your buddy Mark. I will see you and the United Arab Emirates next week."

Eric said, "That's great. I'll have a few surprises for you."

It was Thursday, the day before our flight to the United Arab Emirates.

I said, "Carla and Amber, listen up. Tomorrow Friday we are leaving Washington, D.C., for the United Arab Emirates, so if I were you girls I would get some sleep."

CHAPTER 5

When the Plan Comes Together

The time was 6:30 in the morning. Carla, Amber, and I moved our suitcases out of the room. I whistled for taxis and the taxi arrived. Carla was dressed in her traditional Muslim dress and Hijab, Amber, had a little bit of a problem walking in the Muslim dress called the Abaya, but she got into the taxi okay. The ride to the airport to go around it was around an hour and 20 minutes. I handed Amber and Carla their plane tickets and passports.

When we got into the terminal building of the Royal International UAE airline, we proceeded, to go to the check-in desk at the Ronald Reagan International Airport outside of Washington, D.C. We gave our luggage to the check-in person at the United Arab Emirates Airlines desk. Then we went through a series of metal detectors and were permitted finally to board the plane.

As he got on board, the stewardesses were giving us the passengers a safety briefing and preflight instructions. The plane, after a couple of minutes, started to roll down the runway at the Ronald Reagan International Airport. We took off at 9 a.m., which means that we will be arriving in the United Arab Emirates around 3 p.m.

Carla, Amber, and I set down in our seats at the United Arab Emirates Royal Airlines.

I asked Amber, "Did you bring your CD player on this trip?"

She said, yes I did. As a matter of fact, I have it in my carry-on bag."

I then asked, "You have Arabic CDs?"

"Yes, I also have them in my carry-on bag," said Amber.

"Okay, this is going to be about a 9-to-10-hour flight. In this case, if I were you, I would still try to learn a little bit more of the Arabic language."

Amber said, "Okay Mark."

After the cabin crew went over the safety instructions, the Royal United Arab Emirates Airplane began to taxi and after a couple of minutes, we took off. Amber put on her headphones and began to learn the Arabic language.

We took off from Ronald Reagan International Airport, in Washington, D.C. and we flew for 11 hours, then we landed in the United Arab Emirates in Dubai, to be exact. Carla, Amber, and I grabbed our carry-on luggage, and we headed for the door of the aircraft.

Carla said, "Listen, Amber, from now on you will follow Mark's instructions to the letter."

As we got off the airplane, Carla, Amber, and I headed for the immigration and customs check-in.

I said, "Okay Amber, I'm going to go first through customs."

I approached the immigration check-in desk, and the immigration officer asked, "Is your name Mohammed Aziz?"

"Yes, it is, Sir," I quickly answered.

"Is your visit to Dubai business or pleasure?" he asked.

"Pleasure."

He ran my passport through the database scanner, I waited for a couple of minutes, and he stamped a visa in my passport.

Amber was going through customs next. As Amber approached the immigration and customs officer's desk, she was kinda nervous.

The immigration officer asked her, "Is your name Miriam Khalifa Bin Laden?"

Amber answered in Arabic, "Yes, it is."

Then the immigration officer asked, "Is your visit to Dubai for business or pleasure?"

Amber answered in perfect Arabic, "Pleasure." Then Amber passed through the customs without problems.

Carla was the last to go through the customs and immigration check and because of her experience, she also passed through the customs check without a problem.

We walked to the airport and then I saw my friend Eric.

"Hello, Eric, it is good to see my friend. Amber, by the way, congratulations. You handled yourself very well at the customs and immigration check-in. I'm impressed," I said.

"It is good to see you Mark, let me grab your bags," said Eric.

He grabbed our bags, and we walked out of the airport terminal. Carla, Amber, and I got into Eric's Cadillac Escalade SUV. We drove from the airport through the streets to Dubai for two hours. The streets of Abu Dhabi, the capital of Dubai, looked like you were in the cities of Star Wars; the buildings looked really futuristic. After two hours of driving from the airport, we finally arrived at my friend Eric's house.

Eric said, "You guys better get some sleep because we've got a lot of work to do tomorrow, and Mark, I have a little surprise for you." So after we arrived at my friend Eric's house, we went right to sleep.

The next morning, we woke up, and somebody knocked on the door. My friend Eric went to answer it as Carla, Amber, and I were sitting at a breakfast table. My friend Naseem walked into the dining room.

"Hi Mark, it's good to see you again. I know what happened to you guys. The mission itself was a screwup from the beginning." Naseem pulled out a folder. On the top of the folder, it said TOP-SECRET.

I asked, "Naseem, why are you showing me this stuff?"

"I got into an argument with Mike because he kinda knew about this mission being a setup. Mark, you better have a look at the memo inside the folder," she said.

I opened the folder and started to read the memo.

It said: *Memorandum, it is the policy of the United States not to negotiate with the Palestinians and any of those organizations such as the PLO or Hezbollah, not to negotiate for the release of hostages however, in this case, there will be an exception to the rule, in this case, the crew of the flight R521 is to be exchanged for a Palestinian prisoner that is held by Israel her name is Ana Moon in this exchange shall be complete on August 30, 2023.*

Amber and I said, "We already knew about this."

"But," Naseem said, "You better have a look at the signatures of our senators who have signed off on this person exchange deal."

We looked at the signatures: it said: *Sen. Joe Fishburne, a Democrat, and Sen. Eddie Rocker a Republican.* This exchange will take place on August 30, 2023. However, if this exchange does not happen, then the crew of Flight R521 is to be disposed of.

After careful analysis of the situation, I said, "Okay guys, Amber, we don't have a lot of time to plan for this rescue operation. However, will do our best to get this job done."

As Carla, Amber, and Eric were talking, the doorbell at my friend Eric's house buzzed. My friend Eric went to the door, and as he looked through the peephole, he saw Naseem.

As Naseem walked to the door she said, "Mark, it's great to see you again. I know what happened to you guys in Israel. However, Mark, this was not your fault."

"But Naseem, with your help, Amber's, and Carla's, we will get our guys back, by any means necessary. Okay, we have a lot of work to do. We do not have a lot of time to do it, so let's get to work," I said in an urgent tone.

"What you have there in those envelopes, Naseem?" I asked.

"These are the latest satellite photos of the Bathsheba prison in Israel where our guys are being held. I also have the latest topography and regular maps of the area in question," answered Naseem.

"Okay guys, this operation is not going to be a walk in the park. This will take some major planning. I told Eric to call up Dunkin' Donuts and told them to bring us some coffee and donuts because this is going to be a long day and a long night too." I said.

Then I asked Naseem, "Do you have the most updated blueprints of the facility?"

Naseem looked around. "Here they are," she said.

"Okay, let's go over these blueprints first. Carla, you, and I will cut through the electric fence on the east side of the facility. But before that happens, Naseem and Amber will neutralize the power grid. On the east side, their presence is there. There is a guard tower with one guard that Amber will have to neutralize with her crossbow or dragon-off sniper rifle. Now once that's done, you guys Amber and Naseem get the hell out of the area and find a hole to crawl into and hide.

"Mark, I understand that Amber has to run and hide because she is the least experienced member of this team, but why do I have to run and hide as well?"

"Okay, Naseem, you're coming with me, but Amber, whatever happens after you and Naseem neutralize the east tower and the power grid in the prison; whatever happens, get the hell out of there."

As I looked at the blueprints and the satellite photographs that Naseem had provided for us, I said, "In the middle of the courtyard, there is a manhole that leads into the sewer system from outside. But if we go through the cut in the fence on the east tower before we get to the manhole there will be a minefield that we must crawl through." As I continued looking at the satellite photos, there were at least four helicopters on the other side of the prison for Apache gunships: one and two little birds and two H 60s little birds.

"You're right Mark," said Carla.

"That is our way out, and what is another good thing is that the helipad for those helicopters is right outside of the windows of the cells where our guys, including Captain Ken, are being held."

"Why do I run and hide while you, Carla, and Naseem have all the fun?" Amber asked.

"Amber, please listen to me very carefully. You have been most helpful to this operation with your people skills. You've helped me talk to people to find information. However, this is a strict and very precise military operation. Unfortunately, you are the most inexperienced member of my team." After arguing with Amber for about an hour, I said, "Amber, there's no stopping you because you are just as hardheaded as my old man was; so here is what I'm going to do with you. When we cut a hole in the fence, you're going to stay outside of it with the dragon-off sniper rifle and cover our escape in one of those helicopters. As soon as you hear those engines start, you get the hell out of there and run like the dickens. Don't worry. As soon as we see you running, we will land and pick you up."

"Now let's go through the plan one more time. Noon we take off from Back Car Valley Lebanon and aboard the AC 47 Aircraft. At 12:30, we will reach the drop zone in the Negev Desert and then we will jump out of the airplane. When we get to the prison, Naseem and Amber, what are your jobs?"

Amber answered, "To neutralize the guard tower on the east side so you and Naseem can crawl through the fence and the minefield for you guys to get into the sewer system, and all hell will break loose. I find the prisoners and the helicopter as fast as possible and get out of there. So, for about 2 miles of land, we pick up Amber and immediately fly to the United Arab Emirates. If that's not possible, then we will fly to Saudi Arabia. This is what will happen if the operation is successful; this should not take no more than four hours."

"Naseem, can you contact one of your sources in the Negev Desert and ask them if the prisoners are still being held in the same cells in the Bashiba Prison?"

"Yes Sir, Mark. I can do that right now."

Naseem contacted her friend, who is an Arab Bedouin. His name is Mohammed Abdullah Ibrahim, and he lives in the Negev Desert near the Bashiba Prison.

She asked him on the phone, "Mohammed, this is your friend Naseem."

"Hello."

She asked, "Are the American prisoners still being held in the Bashiba Prison?" Mohammed answered after a couple of minutes.

He said, "Yes they are, but their condition is not so good. One of them walks with the aid of crutches. It looks like he's got a broken and busted knee, and he's always leaning on the dude with the dark hair."

"What is the condition of the dude with the black hair?" Naseem asked.

"He is okay. He limps a little bit."

"What is the condition of the gentleman with the baldhead and glasses?" she asked.

Mohammed answered, "His condition is good but his hand, the right one, is wrapped in a sling. They let the prisoners out three times a day. Those jackasses are building three posts in the prison yard. I think they're going to execute the prisoners in a couple of days. So, in this case, you guys better hurry."

Naseem quickly responded, "Tell your friend Mohammed we will be there before he knows it." After Naseem finished the conversation, my friend Eric pulled out three plane tickets from one of the cabinet kitchen drawers. He also gave us three new passports under the same name.

"The day after tomorrow you guys are flying out to Beirut Lebanon where you will meet a person under the name Anthony Mazor. Anthony will provide you guys with everything you need to carry out this operation, including transportation to your operation zone. This operation will be called Operation Wrath of Saladin, phase 2. Now you guys try to get some sleep because you will have a hard day ahead of you tomorrow."

CHAPTER 6

The Lebanon Adventure

The time was 5:30 a.m., I called Carla and Amber to wake up for breakfast time. As we got ourselves ready, my friend Eric walked into the kitchen.

"Good morning guys, here are your passports and your plane tickets from the United Arab Emirates to Beirut Lebanon, and from Beirut, you guys will go by taxi to the Back Car Valley in southern Lebanon." My friend Eric continued to brief us while we were eating waffles with syrup and toast with butter for breakfast.

"Now your flight from the United Arab Emirates does not leave until noon today. However, have had to wake you guys up early because we have to go over some aspects of this mission. Okay, Mr. Mark, you can take over the presentation for now."

"Okay guys, listen up. We all know that southern Lebanon is controlled by Hamas and Hezbollah."

As I said those words, Amber asked, "Is it true that Hamas and Hezbollah are the top terrorist organizations on the list of the American Central Intelligence Agency?"

"Yes Amber, in this case, you are correct. However, what you have to remember is that nowadays the Central Intelligence Agency in America is not designed to protect the American people from terrorism, it is designed to keep the balance of power in places like the Middle East so that terrorism does not get out of control. Amber, because you know it and I know it that in reality, you are not going to stop terrorism. However, what the CIA does is try to keep a lid on it, that's all."

Carla said, "What a beautiful speech."

"Look Carla, I don't have time for your rivalry things between you and Amber because we still have to get our guys home; so let's stay focused on our job."

As Eric chimed in, he said, "Okay guys, let's go over the part of the plan that will get you guys from here to Lebanon."

"Okay," we said in unison, "let's go over the plan."

"What time does your plane leave from the United Arab Emirates?"

"The plane leaves at noon," I said.

My friend Eric continued with the brief, and asked Carla, "What time do you guys arrive in Beirut, Lebanon?"

Carla answered, "Around 1:30 p.m."

"Now Amber, if somebody in the Lebanon airport asked you what the purpose of your visit is, and what do you do for a living, what do you answer?" Eric asked.

"I am here on the visit to Lebanon because I work with the Ministry of Culture for the United Arab Emirates and I'm here negotiating a deal with the Lebanese Museum of Natural History."

Eric said, "Okay, Amber, you will pass. When you guys get to Lebanon, to the Back Car Valley, a gentleman will pick you up. His name is Chris."

"You mean Chris Bassworth?" I asked.

"Yes Mark, you know him?"

I quickly responded, "Yes I do, Sir. He used to be a weapons instructor when I was initially going through my training in the CIA. Eric, are you telling me that Chris is working for Hezbollah these days?"

"Absolutely, and that is because I think you know why," said Eric.

It was 9:30 a.m., and Amber and I were looking through the maps.

"Okay, Amber and Carla, let's go through the blueprints and the plan one more time. Amber, what is your job?"

"I take out the main tower of the prison and cut through the fence so that Carla and I get in."

"Now listen, Carla will go to get into the prison to get our guys out through the sewer system. The entrance to the sewer is about to be seen from the fence post. Now these little devices that are lying here on the table look like medical band-aids but they are not. Those things contain about 2g of explosives. Now, Amber, you are to remove the controller that looks like a kid's toy car remote control."

Amber said, "Yes."

"You see, the switches?"

"Yes, I do."

"Alright, above each switch, there is a light. Once you power up the switch on the remote control, each of these lights must be green. When each of these lights turns green and I give you the signal hillbilly bang, bang. No matter what's happening around you, the explosives will go off. They will do what they have to do, and no matter what is happening, you run like hell to the desert. Amber do not worry because at that time Carla and I will be getting into one of those helicopters that they keep on the prison grounds for riot control. Once we start those engines, you will be running in the desert. Like I said, do not worry, we will pick you up right outside of the prison in the desert. Now I ask Eric, what kind of helicopters are others keeping their right to control, and are those helicopters armed at all?" I said.

"Yes, the Israeli prison system keeps two Cobra gunships, and they are armed with standard rockets, your standard Cobra Apache package, and they also keep three UHs. One utility helicopter and they are armed with Michigan's in the door and standard rocket packages as well."

"Eric, as of now, are those helicopters fully fueled?"

"Yes, those helicopters are always fueled because they have to be because they use them to control riots in the prison. They also have two or three Stryker armored vehicles that are armed with pepper ball guns and less-than-lethal ports where they can launch gas from and in this prison. They maintain a fully armed security force outside, and also the rest of the prison guards had weapons training as well," Eric said.

I said, "Thank you, Mr. Eric, for such a wonderful briefing and intelligence."

The time was 10 o'clock. I said, "Carla and Amber, let's get packing because we don't want to mess up our flight to Lebanon."

It was 10:30 a.m., and our taxicab was going to arrive at 10:50 so I had 20 minutes.

I asked, "So, Eric, are you coming with us on this mission?"

"No, however, do not worry Mark, everything is arranged, even your pickup from the airport in Lebanon."

It was 10:50 when the taxicab had arrived. As Amber, Carla, and I piled into the taxicab, I said to the driver, "To the airport, please." We drove for an hour to the airport that was located capital of Dubai. After going to the inspection of our team boarded the Air Dubai airplane and we flew to Lebanon.

CHAPTER 7

The Back Car Valley

After a three-hour flight, Carla, Amber, and I arrived at Lebanon International Airport in Beirut. As we got off the airplane, we had to go through customs, in this case, Carla and I did okay and Amber did okay as well, however, it took her a little bit longer because the customs officials took a little bit longer to search her bags; everything turned out fine. I whistled for a taxicab; I paid the driver; we got in and the taxi driver drove us for about 5 to 6 hours to Back Car Valley. As we were approaching the training camp, Amber noticed some green flags flying.

Amber asked, "Hey Mark, are those green flags Hamas flags, and the yellow flag with the hand that is holding the M-16 are those flags from Hamas?

"Yes Amber, those green flags are Hamas and the yellow ones with the M-16 are Hezbollah flags."

As the taxi driver was getting closer to the main gate, the taxi driver was stopped by two men, and Hezbollah masks those men asked for ID. The driver presented them with the ID and they let us pass through.

Amber turned to Carla and said, "Holy Cow, Carla, are you telling me that I'm going to spend five days at that Hezbollah and Hamas training camp?"

"Yes, you are," Carla quickly replied to Amber.

I said, "That's right Amber, if you come on this mission with us, you're going to have to learn some military skills. I know that one week is not going to be ideal for training you. However, one week is at least adequate to teach you some military skills that you will need for this mission."

Amber said, "Oh my gosh, wait till I tell all my friends where I spent my last seven days; one week you're not gonna believe me."

"Amber don't get excited about this now but remember the mission you and Carla are not here on vacation with me you guys are here to help me rescue my crew from an Israeli jail, in which case we do not have a lot of time, so we will have to kinda work quick," I said.

As the taxi driver pulled up to the compound, a Black guy in camouflage gear was waiting there and he did not wear a mask. As the taxi stopped, he opened the door. Amber and Carla got out of the taxicab and I did as well. I was wearing a black Islamic and Carla was wearing a black hair cover. It was the traditional Islamic hijab. The Black guy I knew right away, his name was Fahm.

I said, "Hello Lieutenant Fahm."

"Hey Mark, it is good to see you, and your friends too."

"What's up Fahm? You don't work for the U.S. government any more in our lovely state of Delaware?" I asked.

"Hell no! After our lovely Democrats with the president at the front cut our homeland security needs budget, it was time for me to move on," Fahm said, "Mark, I heard what happened to you guys and your crew. I knew this mission was set up to fail from the beginning, and what's even worse is that you guys are going to be scapegoats for its failure. Now, Mark, Amber, and Carla, please follow me to barracks 5. This barracks has separate locker rooms for four male and female recruits."

Carla and Amber walked into the barracks 5. There were three beds with camouflage green fatigues laid out in the neatly military style.

Fahm said, "Okay ladies, change into camouflage clothing, make your beds, and get your boots on. I will come and get you and take you to our gymnasium."

Fahm and I left the girls so that they could prepare themselves for their training. I went into a separate barracks 3, and I put on the camouflage fatigues, a pair of combat boots, and a black mask. The girls got themselves together, and they put on the military fatigues in would-land camouflage. Fahm and I were wearing camouflage gear plus a black mask. We marched into the barracks 5.

I said, "Ladies, let us take a little stroll to our local gymnasium and we're not gonna walk there, but you're going to run there, and fast."

As we got into the gymnasium, I said, "Amber and Carla stand at attention."

At this time I'm still wearing the camouflage gear, boots, and a black mask, as I take off my mask I said, "Carla and Amber as of right now I am not your father, I am not here to babysit your behinds, I am your instructor. I am not here to wipe your noses. I am here to teach you how to at least act in a combat situation. Now Carla, please step forward. Carla may not need so much drill and instructions but you Amber, you do and you're going to get the full military drill plus some basic military training. That is because you are the weakest and the least experienced member of this team. Now we do not have a lot of time. That is why my friend and I are here Mr. Fahm threw you into this forge with fire and brimstone. Amber do not forget our purpose here. My job, our job, I mean me Mr. Fahm's, and Carla's job is to teach you at least how to survive on the battlefield that we're going into, and don't forget what our purpose for this training is to rescue our friends who are being held in an Israeli jail as of right now. However, they don't have a lot of time and that means we don't have a lot of time to waste because they are counting on us and all on our rescue efforts. So my dear Amber what I suggest you better start learning fast. Now, Amber, this is Mr. Fahm. All this week, he and I will be teaching you hand-to-hand combat and fighting with a knife. Okay, Amber, come forward," I said. As Amber came forward, I handed her a British SAS fighting knife.

"Amber, from now on this is your best friend, this particular knife can save your life. This is the first weapon that you're going to learn how you use and use effectively. Okay, Amber, now watch me. I'm gonna show you your first move and I want to show you what to do with the knife. Amber, this is a cutting and striking weapon," I said. I showed Amber how to use the knife and, to my surprise, Amber was getting the hang of it.

"Amber, congratulations. You have mastered the first weapon that you may have to use during this rescue operation." It was around midnight.

"Amber, it's time for you and Carla to return to the barracks because you'll be starting tomorrow at 7 a.m."

After the girls Carla and Amber returned to the barracks, Amber said to Carla, "I am so tired. I haven't worked out like that since I tried out for the University of Delaware cheerleading squad." Carla said to Amber, "I know this is hard right now, but Amber just thinks about what Carl and the rest of the crew are going through in the Israeli hellhole." After a while, Amber Carla went to sleep.

The next morning at 7 a.m., an alarm bell rang, and I got on the intercom and said, "Okay ladies, you have 15 minutes to do what you have to do, and yet the report and funnier barracks." When Carla and Amber got out of bed in their camouflage fatigues, they stood at attention.

"Ladies let's go for a little run," I said.

As Amber and Carla did the right face, I gave the command to let's start running. We ran about 2 miles, and we ran up to the pistol and rifle range.

I said, "Okay ladies, this is your instructor Drago. He and I will teach you how to operate the latest firearms that you will be equipped with for this mission."

As Amber and Carla approached their respectable tables on those tables, there were the foreign weapons, the Tokarev pistol, your standard AK-47, and your run-of-the-mill PSL Romanian sniper rifle that is based on the Russian drug enough sniper rifle.

"Okay ladies, these are the weapons that we gonna use to rescue our crews. Now Ms. Amber, here is your first rifle that you're going to learn how to use. Okay, Amber, go sit behind a desk; from now on, this is your best friend. I want you to be so familiar with this weapon that you will be able to disassemble and assemble it in your sleep. Instructor Drago will show you how to assemble and disassemble this weapon?"

The instructor Drago began to teach Amber and Carla how to disassemble the PSL sniper rifle, he said, "Step number one is to pull the ball back and check if there is no round in the chamber, step number two is to point the rifle downrange and fire a control shot, remove the top cover, remove the mainspring, remove the bolt assembly in the gas tube and you do the same thing except in reverse order to put the weapon together." I disassembled and assembled the rifle.

Now instructor Drago said, "Okay, Ms. Amber. Now you see how Mark assembled and disassembled the PSL rifle. Now I want you to do it."

Amber made her first mistake by detaching the magazine without pulling the bolt first to check the chamber.

Instructor Drago and I said, "Now Amber, you're doing it wrong. This is not your daddy's 30 x 6 hunting rifle. This is a PSL sniper rifle and first of all, you just violated the number one rule of gun safety."

I said, "Okay Amber, try again."

On the second try, Amber detached the magazine for the bolt and the charging handle back to check the chamber, and she followed all the steps that I and instructor Drago showed her.

"Okay, Amber, the next thing you gonna learn is how to shoot the rifle, Amber, come forward and lie down in a prone position," I said.

"Okay Amber, now this isn't your daddy's 30/06 deer hunting rifle, and this is not West Virginia. I want you to understand the reason I'm teaching you these particular skills with this rifle, because this time we are planning for keeps. Now it is up to us because we have to get your husband and my best friend, Carl, back. Now this PSL rifle is not equipped with the standard Russian scope but is equipped with a red dot." Amber gets behind the rifle and takes a look through the scope.

"You see that red dot? Wherever you point the red dot in the rifle, that's where the bullet is going to go," I said, "okay Amber, detach the magazine." Amber did as I said.

"Amber, here is a box of ammunition and 76 2 x 54. Take one round and put it in the magazine, okay take some more and make sure that all 10 rounds are loaded." Amber did as I said.

"Okay, Amber, put the magazine into the weapon and pull the charging handle back. Now Amber, take a deep breath, put your finger on the trigger, and squeeze gently." When the rifle fired, Amber was happy.

I said, "Congratulations Amber, you even hit right in the middle of the X." Amber was so happy.

"Hey Mark, can I try again?" She asked.

"Be my guest." Amber took aim again and pulled the trigger and the rifle fired again.

"Okay Amber congratulations, you have mastered the second weapon that you're going to use on this mission. Now Amber, let's get back to the shooting table because the next weapon that you're going to learn to use is a 76 2 x 25 Tokarev pistol."

I showed Amber how to use the Russian pistol. When it came to firing the pistol Amber showed remarkable progress. Amber loaded up the magazine with eight shots.

I said, "All right Amber, it is the same thing you did with the rifle except this time you shoot a pistol believing it's easy and squeeze the trigger gently."

Amber pulled the trigger and fired the pistol into the round, landing right in the middle of the target.

I said, "Congratulations, you scored another hit in the middle of the target." Amber got so happy.

She asked, "Mark, can I try again?"

"Go ahead, Amber." Amber fired the pistol again.

"Is it okay Amber firearms training It's almost over. The last weapon you going to learn how to use is a regular 76 2 x 39 AK-47 with folding stock. Amber, now this is the last weapon that you need to learn how to use. The manipulations on this weapon are the same as on the PSL sniper rifle, except for the selector switch. When you push the selector switch on the

AK all the way down, it goes into a single shot. One notch up on full auto and one more notch up is safe. Okay, Amber, get behind the rifle, put the rifle on your shoulder, and fire." Amber fired the rifle, and she was happy.

Amber asked, "Hey Mark, can I do it again?"

"By all means Amber, go ahead." She fired all 30 rounds.

"All right, Amber, you are pretty good with that AK-47 on semi-automatic mode. Now, I want you to flip the switch up one notch to the middle."

Amber did that, and she brought her rifle to her shoulder and pulled the trigger. Since Amber did not have experience firing a full AK-47 with a folding stock on full auto, the rifle started to dance around. Therefore, Amber pulled the trigger all the way and the rifle itself jumped around as bullets were going everywhere.

"Wow! Wow! Amber, get your finger off the trigger!" We all yelled.

After the little mishap that Amber had, I said, "Amber, listen to me, you hillbilly you; this is not your daddy's shotgun, this is a full auto AK-47!"

Amber got really upset, and she yelled at me. She said, "Mark, don't you yell at me. I am not one of your soldiers and you are not a drill instructor! How come she's not drilling here with us?!"

I said, "Amber, Carla does not need all this drilling and training; she worked with me in the CIA in the Special Operations Division for 20 years. So she has the necessary experience and Amber, remember this you are the weakest person on this team. The reason is that you have never done this before and it's okay. It's all right, however, I have to at least get you to be proficient enough so you can come with us on this mission. You want to come with us on this mission, so think about this for now. How are we going to rescue Carl and the rest of my friends? Don't get frustrated with this and yes, I did yell at you, because I want to create another stress level. Remember, we are going into a hostile environment, and if you cannot handle me yelling at you, give you an order, and teach you how to use the equipment and the weapon that is used for this particular mission. In that case Amber, I would seriously consider rethinking whether I want to go on this mission or not. Amber, calm down to pick up the weapon again, and let's try again." Amber gets behind the shooting table and loads 30 rounds into the magazine.

"Now watch me again put the rifle against my shoulder, hit the selector switch to the middle, and fire short bursts like this. Now Amber, try again to hold on to the rifle tight, hold it tight against your shoulder, and squeeze it squeeze the trigger." Amber finally was getting the hang of it. She fired for short bursts.

I said, "All right, Amber, you're getting the hang of it now. Put the rifle against your shoulder, hold on to it tight, and let her long burst." Amber put the rifle on her shoulder and pulled the trigger.

"Okay, Amber, just remember to put the rifle against your shoulder," I said. Amber fired the rifle. She held her rifle, and every bullet landed on the target.

I said, "You see that Amber? Now you get the hang of it." Amber was so happy that she was able to do that.

She said, "Mark I'll try again."

"Go ahead, have fun," I said. She fired the AK-47 a couple more times. She was screaming with happiness, "Yahoo!"

I said, "Now you have learned and mastered another weapon that you will be using on this mission."

It was 5:45 p.m., and I said, "Okay Amber, now you only have one more weapon to master for this mission. It is a crossbow. Now this weapon will not take that long because this is the easiest weapon to learn. Amber, these are Broadhead arrow tips. The crossbow works just like a rifle, but here is how you load it. You put your crossbow down with your foot into the strap, which is an arrow. They crank the crossbow lines to put your arrow and then put the crossbow against disorder like this and just pull the trigger like you would do it on the rifle. Let me show you."

I loaded up the arrow into the crossbow. I put the crossbow against my shoulder and I looked through the scope. As I looked through my target, I saw the X in the middle, which was pulled with the lab screen arrow, left the crossbow, and hit the target.

Amber said, "Mark, this looks like fun. I'll try it."

"Go ahead," I said. Amber loaded up the crossbow with the arrow and found it to be fun.

She said, "This is fun. I'm getting the hang of this fairly quickly."

"All right, Amber, that is enough of practice. Tomorrow you're going to start Jump School." Now, it was about 6 p.m., and I said, "Amber, don't hang out with Carla in the barracks for now and try to get some sleep because tomorrow it's going to be a long day."

CHAPTER 8

The Jump School

The time was 5:30 a.m., I got up and got on the intercom and said, "Ladies, the time is 5:30 a.m., it's time to get up." I walked into barracks number 5 where Amber and Carla were staying.

I said, "Okay Amber and Carla, you have about 20 minutes to pack your gear; that is because you're going to a special place today." As I walked outside barracks number 5, Amber and Carla stood up with their gear, military fatigues, and combat boots.

My friend Fahm pulled up on the bus. He said, "All right ladies, get on board. Today, ladies, you are taking a special field trip."

After we got on board the bus, we rode for about an hour.

"This part of the camp was hosting a Parachute Jump School," Fahm said as we arrived at the site. "Mark and you two girls can get off the bus now."

I said, "Carla and Amber, listen up. Let's walk all the way to the airplane hang." As we walked into the hangar, Amber noticed all those parachutes hanging in the rafters.

"Oh, no Carla, you telling me that I'm gonna have to learn how to jump out of an airplane? A perfectly good airplane at that?" Amber asked Carla.

Carla and I said, "Yes, exactly."

As Carla, Amber, and I walked to the hangar, a friend of mine, Wild Bill. He got to his office and said, "Good morning ladies and gentlemen, I have the honor of being your parachute jump instructor. Now Mr. Mark, Ms. Carla, and Ms. Amber, please take a seat."

As Amber, Carla, and I took seats behind our desks, Wild Bill said, "In this part of training, you will be learning how to jump out of a perfectly good airplane. Now we are not skydivers. In this facility, you will be learning how to make an actual combat jump into hostile territory. You will be making the jump from an airplane at an altitude of 18,000 feet. What you have to learn is that it is very cold. That is why Mr. Mark and Ms. Carla take Ms. Amber to get fitted for a special jumpsuit. Now Ms. Carla and Mr. Mark take Ms. Amber to the pseudo-program and show her all the colors of the jumpsuits she has to choose from." Amber chose a white suit with blue sleeves.

"Okay, Amber," Wild Bill said, "I want you to lay down on the floor and arch your back like this."

As Carla and I were lying on the floor showing Amber the proper way to arch her back, Wild Bill continued, "Amber, this is the proper procedure and the proper way to float with your back arched; so that the air goes around you when you exit out of the airplane. Because after exiting the airplane you will be floating in the air for about 30 seconds until your parachute opens, you will keep your feet together and float down normally."

After hours of practice with me and Carla, Amber was getting the hang of it.

Wild Bill said, "Okay Amber, you and Mark are going for a little run a couple of miles down from the drop zone. There is an obstacle course."

"Okay," Amber and I said.

"Now you will have 15 minutes to run through this obstacle course. Since you are not in great shape and you have never done this before, this will take you an hour. But that's okay because you will run through the obstacle course two times, maybe three, and the reason for this exercise is to strengthen your legs and ankles on your feet. As I said jumping out of the airplane itself is the easy part, but landing it is the hard part. Especially when you've never done it before. So Amber, when you hear the whistle, we will run through this together."

Since Amber had never run through a course like this before, she had a little bit of trouble climbing through the wall.

As I saw that I yelled, "Amber, stop!" I said, "Okay Amber, watch me, put your foot into the crack and hold on to the wall, put your other foot in front of the other one, and swing your legs over." Amber did that.

"Okay," I said, "Amber, the next obstacle you will crawl through in a prone position." Amber did that pretty well; she was almost to three obstacle courses.

I said, "All right Amber you did okay for your first time, however, you have to get through this obstacle course in around 15 minutes," Amber was already tired but I said, "Amber let's try it one more time." Amber and I ran through the obstacle course again. To my surprise, Amber was getting the hang of it.

I said, "Amber, let's go to the gym to lift some weights, especially for your legs, because you have to have some strength training to jump out of the airplane." So me and Amber went to the gym. I was lifting weights and Amber was working out on the leg strength machine.

It was 9 p.m. in Lebanon. I said, "Amber, you did well today but tonight try to get some sleep because tomorrow you, Carla, and I are going to make a practice jump out of an airplane." It was 9:15 p.m. and Amber and Carla went to sleep.

The next morning around 8 a.m., I gave the girls a wake-up call.

I said, "All right ladies, today is your big day. Amber, you're gonna jump out of the airplane for the first time."

Amber and Carla have put on their sweatpants, T-shirts, and a pair of sneakers. Carla, Amber, and I walked into the hangar.

I said, "Amber, this is your jumpsuit." The jumpsuit was white and had blue sleeves. Amber changed into the jumpsuit.

I said, "Here's your helmet for parachute jumping and it looks the same as your motorcycle helmet with the mouthpiece and a plexiglass shield."

I said, "Okay Amber, it is time to put on your parachutes."

When Amber, Carla, and I put on our parachutes with the rest of the gear, and then it was time to walk to the aircraft. The aircraft that we were going to use for this jump was a Jordanian Air Force's C-47 Dakota. Carla, Amber, and I boarded the aircraft, as the engines roared the airplane started to taxi down the runway it started to lift off and the airplane began to fly to the altitude of 18,000 feet where Amber was going to make her first training jump of course. Carla and I accompanied her on this occasion. At this point, Amber was getting scared.

I asked, "Amber, what are you so nervous about?"

She said, "I am scared, that's because I never jumped out of an airplane."

I said, "Look Amber, that's totally natural." As we began to reach the altitude of 18,000 feet, the light on the side of the door on the panel turned red.

Wild Bill said, "Stand up everyone, stand up, everybody count to 1, 2, 3." Wild Bill gave the command to stand in the door.

As I stood at the door, I said, "Carla, Amber, as I stood at the side door,"

Amber, I said, "Prepare to jump." As Amber stood at the door, she got scared when she looked down.

I said, "Amber, don't look down. Look straight ahead, don't look down."

I counted one to three with a big scream, "Yahoo!" Amber jumped out of the airplane, Carla went next, and I jumped last. We all met up in the air. I gave the signal with my hands for us to split.

I said, "Amber 1,2,3 pull the handle." Amber did and then the parachute opened.

She screamed, "Yahoo!" Then the air was really quiet and then we flowed to the ground. Carla landed first, Amber landed second, and I was the last one to land.

As we took off our parachutes, a Humvee arrived and an officer from the intelligence bunker arrived, and said, "Mark, here is a message for you."

As I opened the envelope that contained the message, it was an intercept from the radio spy satellite. It said that the Israelis were torturing one of the crewmembers, named Chris. He was beaten very badly and thrown into a cell full of rats and water.

I said, "Amber, Carla, we have to get back to the operational bunker because there's going to be some changes to the rescue plan."

Amber took our parachutes to the hangar where the Packers got a chance to fold the shoes and prepare them for the next jump or training jump, for that matter.

I said, "Okay Amber, you going to come with us with me and Carla, into the Israeli prison where Carl, Captain Ken, and Chris are being held. Amber pay attention because this is how it's gonna work. Carla and I will crawl through the minefield into the sewer system. We will crawl in first and then you're going right behind us after you neutralize the towers. Amber, when I give you the signal 'bang bang', you set off the explosives and you crawl through the barbwire through the minefield, the main hole jumping to the sewer. When we get out and we find the crew of our plane, now we know that Chris is being held in a cell that is flooded with water and rats.

Amber said, "Excuse me but why do I have to cover your escape? I thought that Carla and I were going to carry Chris out on a stretcher."

I said, "No Amber, and the reason for that is that you know that you and Carla will not be able to carry him for long distances because he is one fat fuck, you see Carla and I will be able to carry him, but you and Carla will not. Besides, when we get on the helicopter, I will need you to take care of the wounded because after Chris, for example, has been held in a cell that is filled with water and rats, he might need some major medical attention. In that case, Amber, you're the best person for this job. Okay, Now Amber and Carla, let's go through the changes to the rescue plan one more time."

"Okay, Amber, what is your job?

"Neutralize the towers, cut a hole in the fence," Amber said.

"Okay, Carla, what's next?"

"You, Amber, and I will crawl to the main hole and get into the sewer system. This will get us into the prison. If we don't raise the alarm, we will go back the same way we came. If not, then we will have to improvise. Open up the cells and let the prisoners out. If Chris is in bad shape, then we will have to get him on a stretcher and will have to carry him out to the helicopter. We will all fly to Jordan, where we will go through the debriefing and then we all can go home to Andrews Air Force Base."

"Now Amber," I said, "we have to get ready for another training jump."

Therefore, Carla, Amber, and I went back to the airplane hangar and put on our parachutes, the equipment such as our weapons, and the equipment that we would need to complete our mission. The airplane engines were already warming up. Our flight crew consisted of two pilots: one name was John and the other was Eddie. We boarded the C 47 and would have closed the door. However, when we were boarding the aircraft, Amber had a little bit of trouble walking with the heavy equipment. Amber, mind you were carrying not only her rifle and her other equipment but she was carrying a portable structure.

The airplane took off and was taking us to 18,000 feet. However, this job was different. Our jump master Wild Bill gave the command for everyone to stand up. We all stood up and the lights on the center panel were red.

Wild Bill said, "Everyone stand in the door."

Amber, Carla, and I walked slowly to the door of the aircraft. The light turned green. Wild Bill said, "Go!"

I jumped first, then Wild Bill kept shouting, "Go! Go!"

Carla jumped right behind me, and Amber jumped last. But this time, even with her equipment, she was not scared to jump out of the airplane. We floated in the air for 10 seconds.

I said to everyone, "One, two, three!" We pulled the parachute handles, and the parachute opened; we floated to the ground safely.

I said, "Okay Amber, not bad." Amber was happy that she was able to make the jump with her extra gear. Carla was also happy, and I was, too.

I said, "Okay ladies, there's one more job that you will have to do. It is your last training jump, and that is a night jump which we will do tomorrow. Right now, let's get our information, grab our shoots, and march to the hangar to put our parachutes down. Let's march toward the barracks and try to get some sleep because tomorrow you will not only have a long day but it's going to be a long night too." It was around 7 p.m., and we were so tired that we went right to sleep.

The next morning around 5:30 a.m., Amber, Carla and I headed towards the gym where the first thing I did was hit the treadmill, and Amber started to work out on the universal exercise machine. After the treadmill, I went to work out on the boxing punching bag.

Amber asked, "Hey Mark, what is on the agenda today?"

"Well Amber, we do have, a lot to do, because you and Carla will have a practice night jump and then the real show will get underway. We will get your husband Carla, my best friend, and your brother back. Don't you worry about that?" We spent about 5 to 6 hours in the gym where Carla and Amber practiced hand-to-hand combat and we worked out on the exercise machines.

The time was 6:30 p.m., and the dusk started to fall on the training camp Back Car Valley in Lebanon.

I said, "Okay ladies, this is our final training jump. It is a night jump, so in this case, we will have to be very careful. This is because the rescue operation of the flight crew of R521 will take place at night, so that's why this jump is so important."

As Amber, Carla, and I began to load up our gear. Amber got loaded up with the regular AK-47 with a folding stock, a 76 2 x 25 Tokarev pistol, and a crossbow, a PSL 76 2 x 54 sniper rifle. Everyone on my team was carrying the same weapons, except Amber was carrying the 76 2 x 54 sniper rifle, and we did carry a survival knife.

As we got loaded up with all of our gear, we marched to the C 47 Jordanian Air Force aircraft that we rented from the Jordanian Air Force. As each of us climbed on board, the engines started to revel up, and we took off for our jump altitude of 18,000 feet.

I said, "Okay ladies, make sure when you guys jump that you have your strobe lights and helmets turned on."

We turned on our strobe lights as we were sitting in our seats and waited for the plane to reach the jump altitude. Wild Bill was the jump master for this training mission as well. Suddenly, the light on the side of the door turned red.

Wild Bill said, "Everyone, please stand up."

We all stood up, and Wild Bill gave the command to everyone, "Please stand at the door."

We were still fine, but suddenly the next light turned green.

Wild Bill asked, "Mark, are you ready?"

"Yes," I said.

He asked again, " Okay, Mark, are you ready?"

"Yes, Sir."

Wild Bill said, "Go!" I jumped out of the airplane, Amber jumped, and the last person to jump out of the airplane was Carla. We all jumped into the night.

I said, "Okay guys, on my mark 1, 2, 3 and we pulled our ripcords that opened our parachutes and then we floated down and were quiet after the jump."

Amber was so happy she screamed, "Yahoo! Mark, this was unbelievable!"

"Yes Amber, you made your first nighttime parachute jump. Now we are ready to bring our friends home."

After we did our jobs, I said, "Guys, let's go look at the blueprints and the model of the present one more time, because we will have to revise some of our operational plans."

Around 9:00 p.m. I said, "Okay guys, let's go meet up in the operations building. My friend Fahm has already set up the model and gave us all the necessary blueprints of the present and its sewer system. Okay everybody, let us look at this model of the prison one more time."

Amber asked, "Mark, why can't we walk in through the front door and disguise ourselves as Israeli, Correctional Officers and walk out with the guys?"

"That is a good idea, Amber. However, what we are going to do is go through the minefield, because the guards will not expect this. They don't think anybody is crazy enough to go through the minefield. Now, guys, everyone listen up. We will go through this plan one more time so that everyone knows where they're supposed to be and what they are supposed to do."

"Amber, what are you going to do? Are you gonna crawl through the minefield like me and Carla?"

Amber answered, "No, I will be waiting for you guys to go through the minefield so you guys can get to the manhole of the sewer that will lead you into the cellblock, where our guys are being held."

I said, "Okay Amber, what is the code word for you to set off all the explosive charges that Carla will plant on those prison guard towers?

She said, "When you Mark give the word Amber 'bang bang,' that is when I will set off all the explosive charges and then I will follow you guys to the sewer system."

I said, "Okay Amber, now we will walk through the sewer systems for 550 feet and get into the exit manhole. But before we even open the sewer manhole in the cellblock, Carla will have to neutralize the motion sensor that the prison officials have installed. If someone tries to break the prisoners out through the sewer system, what about the way Carla figured out how to break through their motion sensor and open the manhole from outside? Now if we go in silently will go back the same way we came in, but the biggest problem Carla may anticipate is carrying Chris on the stretcher because according to our intelligence reports, Chris was tortured so badly by the Israelis, that he's got a broken leg and gangrene set in so, in this case, will have to give him an injection of antibiotics and get him onto a helicopter that will steal from the prison and whatever happens we will have to fly Jordan as fast as we can. Okay, guys, Carla and Amber return to your barracks and try to get some sleep because tomorrow is the big day when we get our guys back."

CHAPTER 9

Rescue of R521

The time was 11:30 a.m., and Amber and Carla slept in separate barracks. Anyway, I decided that I was sleeping until noon. Amber and Carla were tired after all that training because tonight we were gonna fly the mission to rescue our guys and bring them home.

After I woke up at noon, I took a shower and I thought that I was going to join Carla and Amber at a pickup basketball game on the training base. So Carla and Amber played basketball until 3 p.m.

I said, "Okay girls, the fun is over, and the real mission is about to begin." Amber, Carla, and I walked to the aircraft hangar where our gear was stored. Amber, Carla, and I changed into camouflage clothing.

"Okay guys, let's go and look at this model of the prison one more time. I understand that we've been through this so many times, but let's make sure that everything will go right, and let's look at those prison blueprints and the blueprints of the sewer system. Amber, your job on this mission is to cover our backs because Carla and I will be caring for Chris. So I'm going to need you to cover our backs because me and Carla will have our hands full. Now the most difficult part will be getting Chris into the sewer and to the manhole. We're gonna run through the sewer system as you can see the ways we can go," I said.

The last is a little gate at the end of 150 yards that leads to the back to prison where they're keeping the UH One Helicopter and the two modified Cobra Gunships. Now, whatever happens, I know that particular gate is probably rusted shut. However, I will definitely try to help you guys burst through it. But whatever happens, we have to get Chris, Carl, and Captain

Ken onto that UH One Helicopter because this helicopter has plenty of room for the stretcher. Now Carl has a broken ankle and a few busted ribs. Captain Ken has a couple of broken fingers and also a busted ankle. Chris was in the worst shape because he was the co-pilot of the spy plane under the code name R521. Therefore, Chris will require some medical attention, which is why it is imperative that we get our guys on the helicopter and take off into the night in 15 to 20 minutes.

Now ladies, if everything goes right, then we will go out of the prison the same way we came in. But if Chris plants himself, we will have to take him and, whatever happens, get his ass on a helicopter. Now Carla and I are the two strongest people that can do this, you see.

Amber, I originally was gonna let you stay out outside just to take out the two guards and those towers and destroy all four of those towers with the remote-control detonator. You originally were to run like hell into the desert and try to reach the Jordanian border on your own. However, I had to modify the plan so, in this case, me and Carla will carry Chris on a stretcher and you're gonna watch our backs. Are you okay with it?"

"Let's get on with it," Amber said.

The time was 7 p.m. and the sun was going down. Amber and Carla got to the table, where our gear such as Amber's crossbow, her PSL rifle, my AK-47, and Amber's weapons, which included the same weapons as my weapons, were laid out on the table. We packed our gear, and we started to walk towards the aircraft from the hangar. This aircraft was a D.C. 3 Dakota with the Jordan Air Force markings on it.

Amber was carrying so much gear and equipment that she had a little bit of trouble getting into the aircraft.

I said, "Okay Amber, put your foot on the step below the door. Amber did that."

I said, "Okay, give me your hand and I will pull you onto the plane."

Amber grabbed my hand and Carla pulled Amber into the aircraft. Carla, Amber, and I set in our seats. The two pilots for this mission were Cmdr. John and Cmdr. Robert who was working on a contract with the Jordanian Air Force.

It was 7:30 the dusk was setting in and our airplane took off into the night.

On board the aircraft it was quiet, Amber finally began to speak she said, "Mark you have no idea how happy I am to be going with you guys on this mission to help bring our friends home that the United States government has forgotten about."

"Amber, I am happy that you're here with Carla too but until we are in the air and fly back to Jordan with our guys, I would not start jumping up and down yet."

"I know," said Amber.

We flew for about one hour when one of the red lights started to flash and the jump master Mario said, "Everyone stand up, stand in the door."

As we approached the Israeli airspace, a couple minutes later as we walked to the door, as our jump master Mario opened the door, the light turned green and I was the first person to jump. Amber followed right behind me and Carla jumped last. The night was fairly quiet as we floated down our parachutes; we landed in the middle of the Negev desert fairly close to the Bathsheba Prison.

I said, "Okay guys, we are about two miles from the prison where our guys are being held. We will march at night and in about 2 to 3 hours will be there. Carla and Amber, let's start walking."

We walked for about four hours. It was 11:30 a.m., and the sun was getting hot. We walked for another couple of minutes, we finally reached the Bathsheba Prison.

Amber said, "Okay, Mark, let's go and get these guys."

"Amber, you and Carla get behind the sand dune." Carla and I pulled out our binoculars.

"There about two guards in the tower with a 50-caliber machine gun on each of them plus there is a minefield that goes all the way to the sewer entrance plus on the inside of the prison the Israelis have a tactical response team," Carla said.

So I said, "Okay ladies, gather around, Here is what we're going to do. We will hide here behind the sand dune we will hit this place during the night. So sit tight and watch what's going on for now." As Carla and I were watching what was going on in the prison, we noticed that the barbed wire fence was electrified."

"Okay, genius, how do you plan to get us through the electrified fence?" Carla asked.

"Okay Carla, here is what will do," as Carla and I look through binoculars, "You see that guard tower, the third one on the left? When Amber takes out the guard with her crossbow, you and I will cut through the fence and sneak in through the minefield," I replied.

"But," Carla asked, "Mark, how do you plan to turn off the electrified fence?"

"Okay, Carla, this is what we're going to do. Amber has a backpack with a laptop. On that particular laptop, there's a program that will initiate a computer virus that will disable the electricity grid throughout the whole prison, but the power only stays off for 20 minutes. After that, it comes back on and the electrified fence will also come back on. Carla and Amber listen up. Once Amber activates her laptop and initiates the electrical shutdown virus program starts taking the main guard tower, which is on your left. At that point, Carla and I will head for the sewer manhole. I will set up the explosive charges on some of the towers and I will try to take out some of the military vehicles. Then, after you set the explosive charges off with the remote control, you have to crawl like hell and get to the entrance of the sewer because we will run through the sewer. We will come out of the other manhole right in the middle of the cellblock where the guys are being held. There's a possibility that we might be picking up one extra person who's in the same prison. He is in the same block where our guys are being held to pick up that Palestinian journalist, her name is Anna Moon." Carla and Amber argued for a little bit.

Amber said to Carla, "Carla, let's go get our guys now!"

"Amber and Carla, listen up. We're gonna sit here and nobody is going anywhere until nightfall, because doing this mission in bright daylight is not going to work. It would be suicide so we will and await until nightfall; you ladies got that?" I asked.

Carla said, "All right Mark, we will do this your way."

The time was around midnight. I said, "Okay Amber and Carla, let's try to get closer to the electrified fence. Amber tried to stand up and walked to the electrified fence."

I said, "No Amber, what we're gonna do is we will try to crawl down there, okay Carla and Amber?" Carla and Amber stayed on my heels, we crawled on our stomachs very close to the electrified fence.

I said, "Okay Amber, open up your laptop." Amber went into her backpack and pulled out a Dell laptop.

I said, "Okay Amber, attached to your laptop computer is a disk labeled Ice Nine." When Amber pulled out the laptop, the disk was attached to the laptop's monitor. I said, "Okay Amber, open the DVD drive and insert the disk." Amber did.

I said, "Okay, wait for the program to load." The program has loaded.

"Okay, here's your interface; Amber, click on the Internet connection. Once that happens, you will see that you are connected to the network," I said.

"Okay."

"Okay, Amber, now type the following code letters W594 R." Amber did that.

"Click on okay and watch what happens," I said.

Amber clicked the okay icon on the interface. The entire electric grid went down in 15 minutes.

"Okay, Amber, you stay here," I said. "Carla, follow me." Carla and I crawled to the fence.

"Carla, the power grid is down. Let's cut a hole in the fence." I pulled out the cutting tool, and I cut the hole in the fence.

I said, "Okay Carla, stay on my heels, okay, here we go." Carla and I crawled under the fence.

Suddenly Carla said, "Mark, you are in the middle of the minefield."

"Okay, don't panic."

I pulled out the survival knife and started to feel around the minefield so that I could make a path for myself and Carla and later on so that Amber could cross. As we crawled through the minefield, I was digging with my survival knife so that I could get us through to the minefield safely. I did that. After 10 minutes of crawling through the minefield, Carla reached the manhole that led us into the sewer.

I said, "Okay, let's push this manhole open," Carla and I were trying to get the sewer manhole open, "Carla, stop for a minute."

As I looked up, the surveillance reflector was scanning the area. However, this reflector was attached to the prison building, and it was controlled from the inside because the main power was out. Due to the computer hack that Amber and I did earlier, it took the reflector two seconds to shut down as well. This reflector was controlled from the inside of the prison's security booth.

I said, "Okay Carla, let's open up the sewer manhole." The manhole cover was so heavy but Carla managed to get it open. I went into the sewer first then Carla followed.

As Carla and I got into the sewer, I said on the radio, "Amber, bang bang."

Amber knew that the codeword 'bang bang' meant that she could start taking out the guard towers with her crossbow and the PSL sniper rifle in which case Amber took out three towers with her crossbow and two more were PSL sniper rifles.

I said, "Okay Amber, good job."

Seconds later, as Carla and I were running through the sewer, we heard a bunch of explosions. Therefore, Carla and I knew that Amber had set off the explosives that we planted earlier on those guard towers and a few military vehicles.

I asked Amber, "Can you see the manhole of the sewer through the fence? Do you know where Carla and I went into the prison yard, and how we crawled towards the sewer manhole?"

"Yes, Mark."

I said, "Okay, listen to me. Now crawl down the same path through the fence that Carla and I did going through the minefield footprints."

"Yes, I can see them."

I said, "Okay, follow the same footprints and handprints all the way to the sewer manhole, don't go to the left or the right, stay right on top of those footprints because if you don't follow this path whether you go right or left you might step on the mine. Just follow the path that Carla and I took her earlier." Amber crawled to the minefield, and she managed to get into the sewer.

We heard somebody coming into the sewer. I said in a quiet voice, "Hey Amber, is that you?"

"Yes, you guys, it's me."

After Amber caught up to us, I said, "Okay Amber, whatever happens now when I'm in a slowdown, we have to run like hell. The sewer to the manhole will put us right into the cellblock where our guys are being held." We ran for about 15 to 20 minutes.

We finally reached the manhole that let us outside right in the middle of the cellblock.

I said, "Okay Carla and Amber, I'm going to climb up first because I will have to disable the motion sensor that was placed there because those

Yazd thought that no one would get in through the sewer system." After about two minutes, we reached the manhole that let us into the main cellblock where our guys were being held.

"You to stay here and cover my back," I said.

As I began to climb to open the manhole cover, I noticed that there was a motion sensor. I took my multi-tool out of one of my pouches that I had attached to my bulletproof vest, and I cut the motion sensor power supply, which in my case, disabled the sensor.

I said, "Okay guys, Amber, and Carla, as soon as I leave the manhole cover we're going to have to start moving really fast because there is one guard that is sitting behind the desk. Don't worry, I will take him out, but then, after that, Carla will have to move fast. You got it?"

"Okay Mark, I got it," Amber quickly replied.

I said, "Okay Amber, on three we're going to move this manhole cover." On the second count, I pulled my TT33 pistol out of my holster.

"Okay Amber, lift the manhole cover now."

Amber helped me lift the manhole cover out of the sewer hole in the middle of the prison block. The guard was still sitting at his desk as Amber helped me lift the sewer manhole cover. I climbed out of the sewer, fired two shots from my TT33 pistol, and took out the guard. However, before I managed to take out the guard with my two shots, the guard managed to set off the alarm.

The alarm horn went off. I said, "Okay Amber and Carla, this is where this is going to get hairy."

As the alarm sounded I said, "Carla and Amber, you guys here is what we are going to do. I will go and try to open up as many of the cells. Amber, you will cover us with your AK-47." As Carla and I climbed out of the sewer, Amber followed.

I started shouting, "Carl, Captain Ken, Chris!" Carl was sitting in his cell.

He said, "Mark, I'm here!"

The voice next to Carl's cell shouted, "Can you get us out of here?!"

I quickly replied, "Okay, Carl, step back from the door." I took a patch that looked like a band-aid but it was filled with explosives.

"Okay, Carl, step back from the door."

I put the patch on the door lock and I used the lighter to light and set off the explosives that breached the cell door. After 30 seconds, there was a small pop and the lock of the cell door was broken. Carl could not believe it.

I asked Carl, "Can you walk?"

"I think so. My ankle is busted but I can manage."

I said, "Okay."

Captain Ken was in the next cell to Carl's. I took out another patch filled with explosives so that I could breach the door of the cell. I lit the fuse after 30 seconds and another explosive with a pop sound breached another lock of the cell and I saw Captain Ken.

I asked, "Sir, are you okay? Can you walk?"

"My shoulder is a little busted up, but I think I can manage."

I said, "Okay, I'll be back."

Helping Chris was a little bit different, that is because Lt. Chris was in the worst shape. After all, he was the most tortured by the Israeli interrogator.

I said, "Okay, hang on Chris, Carla and I will get you." Lt. Chris was put in the water-flooded cell with rats in it.

I said, "Hang on Chris."

Another patch with explosives onto the door, and with another small pop, the prison cell where Lt. Chris was being held was breached. Amber covered us with her AK-47.

I said, "Amber, get over here with the stretcher. Okay, Chris, it's me, Mark. I am here to get you out."

As Amber rushed over with the stretcher, I pulled Chris out of the flooded cell with water and rats. Chris's medical situation was really bad because Chris was being held in unsanitary conditions and his right leg smelled bad because gangrene was setting in. As Amber and I were with Chris on the stretcher, Carla was providing cover fire for our escape. The good thing about it is that in all this chaos, Captain Ken and Lieut. Carl managed to grab a Galil rifle and Captain Ken tended to grab one of the guard's 9 mm oozes. Amber and I managed to put Chris on the stretcher.

While all the gunfire was going on, I said, "Okay guys, we will get Chris out to the same sewer system that we came in and watch Chris's head." Carla and Amber managed to get Chris down from the sewer.

I said, "Okay, Carla and Amber, you guys carry Chris on the stretcher and don't look back. Don't worry about us we'll catch up to you."

So Carla and Amber carried Chris on a stretcher. Carl, Captain Ken, and I were running through the sewers, and the security team was throwing gas grenades and concussion grenades at the source. We ran about 500 feet when we caught up to Carla and Amber.

Carla asked, "Okay, genius, which way we go now?"

The grenades were still being thrown into the sewers by the Israeli Special Security squad from the prison.

I said, "Okay guys, we go through the right tunnel."

Amber, Carla, Carl, and I ran about 15 feet, in which case ran into a rusted gate that was locked by a padlock. This particular gate led us out of the sewer pipe, right outside of the prison helipads. Now, in this case, the main concern was the Lieutenant Commander's leg because we were worried that gangrene was setting in. Carla and Amber carried Lieutenant Commander Chris on a stretcher, all the way up to the helicopter, while I was providing cover fire with my AK-47. I had three clips left in a pouch on my bulletproof vest.

As Carla and Amber helped load Chris on a stretcher onto the helicopter, I said, "Okay Amber, you stay in the back with Chris and Carla, you go sit up front in the second seat as my co-pilot."

As I got into the helicopter UH1 cockpit, I began the startup procedures. There was one more prisoner who managed to escape the chaotic situation. Her name was Anna Moon. As Amber was pushing the door of the room cabin of the UH1 to close it, Anna Moon managed to get on board when Amber yelled, "Hurry up!" Amber managed to grab Anna's hand and pulled her into the helicopter.

As the blades started to move to rotate, I asked, "Is everybody okay?"

Then, under fire from the Israeli prison security forces, we took off. We were flying in the air for a couple of minutes. Carl and Captain Ken were okay, except Captain Ken had a broken shoulder and Carl had a broken ankle, but Lieutenant Commander Chris was in worse shape because his leg was infected with gangrene. However, Amber gave Cmdr. Chris a shot of penicillin.

As we were flying through the air Carl shouted, "Son of a bitch, there are two Israeli Apache gunships on our tail."

"Okay, Carl, can you move? Can you get on the 50-caliber machine gun in the door?" I asked.

He said, "Yeah I can move."

I said, "Okay Carl, get on the gun and give them hell."

Carl was firing the 50-caliber machine gun. However, one of the Israeli Apache gunships managed to get us in the tail rotor.

As we were flying through the air, I said, "My pedals feel kind of loose. Look guys, that is the border. We were very close to the Jordanian border. We are going to have to walk there. Amber and Carla, listen up. You guys will have to carry Chris on the stretcher. Okay, guys, I have to put this baby down." I landed the helicopter very gently on the sand next to the sand dunes. The Jordanian border was 1 mile away.

I asked, "Captain Ken, can you walk? Lieut. Cmdr. Carl, can you walk?"

"Yes, we can probably manage."

I said, "Okay, Lieutenant Commander Carl and Captain Ken when I give you the signal you guys had for the border of Jordan like there's no tomorrow, and don't look back. As me and Carla exit, we exit the smoking helicopter. Okay, Carla and Amber, that means you to take Chris and make a run for the Jordanian border as fast as you can."

Amber said, "Carl, you and Carla can carry Chris to the border. I'm staying behind to help Mark."

I said with a stern voice, "Amber, no you're not, you're going with them to the border, I mean it!"

However, Amber, because she was stubborn, said, "Carla and Carl, you guys carry Chris to the Jordanian border." Chris is in bad shape.

"If Mark and Amber will have to stay behind so that the rest of you can get away, I am staying with them, too."

I said, "Okay, you two. Amber, you stay with me, Chris, you too, but the rest of you, that includes you Carl, Carla, and Captain Ken, you guys are going to the Jordanian border and that is it."

Amber and I carried Chris on a stretcher and we put Chris behind the sand dune, as we heard the clicking of the Markerba2 tank tracks and other vehicles. When we knew that the Israelis were right on our tail, we managed to hide Chris on a stretcher behind the sand dunes.

"Okay Chris, here is my TT33 pistol. If you see any of those jackasses come around those corners, you know what to do," I said.

"Mark, don't worry about it. I will handle that."

As the tank and other Israeli military vehicles were getting closer and closer, Amber and Carla asked me, "Okay, Mark, what do we do now? Do we run or fight?"

I said, "Okay guys, here's the situation. We are being surrounded by the entire Israeli division, so running is not an option. So here's what we're going to do. Amber, how many magazines do you have for your AK-47?"

"I only got two left."

I asked Carla the same question. "How many magazines do you have?"

"I have three."

I said, "Okay, I've got two left myself. So here's what we're going to do. We have no choice but to fight. Okay, guys, one more thing. How many grenades do you have?"

Amber said, "I got four left."

"Carla?"

"I've got two."

I said, "I've got three left, but that's okay because here's the plan. Carla, you are going to stay here. Amber and I are going to try to get closer to one of those tanks."

Those things and armored personnel carriers got close to us, then suddenly we heard an Israeli Apache gunship flying overhead. The helicopter hovered over the Israeli military vehicles and through the loudspeakers; we heard somebody speaking in a sort of broken English with a Russian accent.

The Apache pilots said, "Attention the criminals down below. We will not hurt you if you do not run. You are surrounded, you have no chance of escape, you will be given a fair trial."

A few seconds later, the pilot of the Apache gunship helicopter repeated the same ultimatum with the addition of firing warning shots above our heads.

Amber asked, "Okay Mark, what now?"

"Amber, watch this."

I took two of my grenades and I unscrewed the fuse that was connected to the spoon and the pin. I dumped the explosive material on the grenade and screwed the entire component back into the grenade.

Amber asked, "Okay, Mark. What are you planning to do?"

"Okay, Carla and Amber, watch and learn. Amber, see if you can pop off a few rounds from your AK-47 towards that tank. Carla, you back her up." Amber and Carla bumped off a few rounds towards the Mark Aba tank, and the tank started moving towards us.

I said, "Okay Carla, okay Amber, lay down on your stomach as flat as you can."

That tank rolled over on top of us. I pulled the pins of the empty grenades and I threw them inside the tank through the emergency exit hatch at the bottom of the tank. As I threw the grenades, the entire tank crew ran out through the emergency hatch at the bottom.

I said, "Okay Amber and Carla, come on, you guys. Carla, Amber, and I crawled through the same emergency hatch at the bottom of the tank and took over the tank.

Amber and Carla both asked, "Okay, Mark, can you drive this thing?"

"I guess we're going to find out pretty soon."

As I crawled towards the driver's seat, Carla was sitting next to me in the radio operator and the internal machine gun position as well, and Amber set behind me in the loader of the main gun position.

I said, "Okay Amber, you see that thing that looks like a small closet? You push that button and see what happens." The door of the loading magazine opened.

I said, "Okay, Amber. Take one round and put it into the main gun." Amber did what I said.

"Okay, Amber, close the breach." Amber did that.

"Carla, get on a gun," I said. I started up the engine and started moving towards the Israeli tanks and armored vehicles.

I said, "Amber, when I give you the signal, you fire that round." As I was speeding with the tank towards the Israeli military vehicles and Carla was firing the M2 40 machine gun, I said, "Amber, fire now!"

As Amber pulled the lanyard that fired the main gun, all we heard was a giant clank of the main gun. We heard the explosions that hit one of the Israeli armored vehicles that was in front of us in the row that was surrounding us.

The Apache gunship pilot said, "One more time please, stop the tank! If you stop, no harm will come to you." He fired the same rounds into the tank; we could hear many gun bullets bouncing off the tank's armor.

I said, "Okay Amber, raise the gun barrel of the meeting gun about 90° and put another round into the breach." Amber took another round from the magazine and put the round into the chamber.

Amber closed the breach and said, "Ready."

I said, "Okay Amber, put the main gun on a 90° angle because we're going to take out that helicopter." Amber did that.

I said, "Okay."

As I was speeding and wrecking the entire Israeli, the column was breaking up and there were some very big piles of burning Israeli tanks and other vehicles.

I said, "Okay Amber, fire!" Amber pulled the lanyard again, and the gun fired. We hit the helicopter but the pilot still was coming at us.

I said, "Okay, Amber, one more round."

"Mark, there is no more ammunition."

I said, "Okay, Carla, how much ammo do you still have in the 240 machine gun?"

"I'm down to my last belt."

I said, "Okay, here's what we're going to do. I am going to ram that helicopter as he gets closer to the ground and we will stop firing for four minutes."

The Apache gunship was hovering very close to the ground. I gave the tank full gas, and we rammed that helicopter with everything we'd had. We destroyed the helicopter by ramming it.

I said, "Okay guys, we're going to get out of the tank the same way we got in through the emergency hatch at the bottom."

Suddenly, we heard on the radio, "Hello, Hello this is the Royal Jordanian Air Force jets. What are your intentions?"

At that time Israeli jets were flying towards us because they were going to destroy the tank that we captured and rammed that helicopter. The Jordanian Air Force jet was piloted by my Maha. I heard Maha's voice on the radio.

I said, "Maha, is that you?"

"Yes Mark, it's me; now get your friends out of the tank because there is a world of hurt coming down."

We ran out of the tank to the emergency hatch at the bottom, as the Jordanian Air Force was trying to protect us from the Israelis. A Jordanian military medevac helicopter landed Carla, Amber, Captain Ken, Carl, Chris, and I got on board the medevac helicopter and a helicopter took us to the Jordanian Military Hospital where my crew and I spent three months in recovery.

CHAPTER 10

The Consequences of Our Actions

We were flowing to the Jordanian Military Hospital on the medevac chopper when Carl, Chris, Carla, and Amber yelled, "Yahoo we're going home, all of us!"

Chris, Carl, and Captain Ken were celebrating. However, Captain Ken said, "You guys, I am glad that you are happy, but you have to realize that it'll be hell to pay for Mark for putting this operation together."

As we landed on the roof of the Jordanian Military Hospital, Chris was rushed into an emergency exam room. After a couple of hours, Chris was placed in a regular hospital room. Carl, Carla, Amber, Captain Ken, and I after our medical examinations, were all placed into regular hospital rooms.

A couple of days later as I was resting in the hospital bed. A U.S. Marine came into my room. He said, "Captain Mark?"

"Yes Sir."

"I am Gunnery Sgt. Ramos from the Judge Advocate General Office, you have been charged with the violation of the U.S. National Security Act. You better get yourself a lawyer."

After a while, Lieutenant Chris came to visit me in my hospital room.

He asked, "Mark, who was that?"

"Chris, unfortunately, I have some bad news. That was Sgt. Ramos; he was from the Judge Advocate General Office, it appears that I'm going to be charged with the violation of the American National Security Act."

Chris thought about it for a couple of minutes. He got and he said, "You gonna be charged?"

I said, "Yes Chris, I'm going to be charged with a violation of the

American National Security Act and the only reason to charge me with that is that I have decided to get you guys home, and I did not go through the proper channels because I knew that this was a lot of work."

A couple of minutes later, Carl came into my hospital room. He asked, "Hey Mark, what is going on?"

"That Marine was Sgt. Ramos, he's from the Judge Advocate General Office and he said I've been charged with a violation of the American National Security Act because I got you guys back home."

"This is impossible, also we better get you a lawyer. I'm going to call my father to see if he knows anybody with a military background and who has a license to practice military law," Carl said.

After a few weeks in the Jordanian Military Hospital, I was handcuffed, put on a plane, and flown to Fort Leavenworth military discipline barracks in Kansas. I was placed in the Fort Leavenworth Kansas Military Disciplinary Barracks for about three months until my case was going to trial. While I was there, I met a good friend of mine Andy when I started my job in the CIA in the antiterrorism division. He was working there as a prison guard. Because of my knowledge and high military status, I was placed in solitary confinement for the duration of my preliminary detention.

The next morning Amber came to see me. Andy, one of the prison guards, unlocked me and said, "Mark, you have a visitor." As I was being led to the visitor room, I saw Amber through the plexiglass so I picked up the receiver of the phone that was hanging on the wall.

Amber picked up her phone and said, "Hi Mark, how are you holding up?"

"I'm doing okay under the circumstances," I said.

"Mark, I got you a lawyer. He is flying in tomorrow at noon to see you. His name is Lieutenant Commander Joseph McNealy, and he will be handling your defense in Your court martial."

I asked, "Amber, tell me the truth. How are the kids and Carla handling the situation?"

"They're okay, but do not worry about that right now. I have some things for you."

Amber gave me a package, I took the package that Amber gave to me, and in that package, there was one of my favorite things which was an Italian cheesesteak with a bottle of Coca-Cola. Amber also sent me my dress uniform so that I would look presentable for my trial.

After three months I spent in solitary confinement because of my alleged crimes, I got myself dressed up, was placed in the military police van, and driven to the courthouse. But what I did not expect was that as the convoy was approaching the courthouse, there were so many reporters with cameras, including the major TV networks such as CNN and NBC, CBS, and Fox News. As I was being let out of the police van with my attorney, Joseph McNealy surrounded by a crowd of reporters. However, in that particular crowd, I saw Amber and Carla and all my friends that I went to Wilmington High School with. I was let into the courtroom and on the cuffs for my handcuffs and my attorney Joseph sat down at the defendant's table. I saw one of the naval officers walk into the courtroom and sit down at the table that was meant for the prosecution.

In two minutes we heard the words, "All rise, the case against Captain Mark is being presented by the Honorable. Lieut. Paul McDougall presiding." Everyone stood up and sat down.

After a couple of seconds, Judge Paul said, "Would the prosecution care to make an opening statement?" The prosecuting attorney, whose name was Iola Fienberg, began to speak.

She said, "What we have here is a total disregard for authority and the chain of command. We also have the case of negligence and irresponsibility of superior officers and total disregard of our constitutional law."

The judge asked, "Captain Mark, how do you plead?"

"Not guilty Your Honor."

The judge in that case said, "I will declare a short recess and we will resume the trial at 2 p.m..

As everyone left for lunch, I still sat at the defendant's table as my friends came to see me. One of my friends with whom I went to Wilmington High School with Joe said, "It is good to see you. How you're holding up?"

"I'm doing okay. I will do even better after this is all over," I said.

"Whatever happens here today, Mark, I want you to know that you pulled the most spectacular military operations ever devised, and whatever happens, you will always have your friend's support."

At 2 o'clock, the trial resumed, and the lawyer for the prosecution said, " Here is 'Exhibit A' which will show that Captain Mark disobeyed a direct order of not getting involved any further in the rescue of the crew of the flight known as R521. The prosecution has produced a document, a nondescript closure agreement that specifically stated that under no circumstances Captain Mark was going to get involved in rescue operations of such proportions without prior authorization. Captain Mark also signed the nondisclosure agreement and agreed not to discuss any operations of national security significance of even his family members, and I do have evidence sufficient to charge Captain Mark with the violation of the National American Security Act." At that point, the prosecution was finished with the opening statement.

Next, my defense attorney began to speak. He said, "I do not doubt what the prosecution said here today. However, I have evidence to prove that Captain Mark has opted in good faith and honor by bringing these men home to their families. Meanwhile, the U.S. government allowed its own man brought to a foreign prison under very difficult conditions."

The trial lasted for three hours, the prosecution was given evidence and Captain Mark's defense attorney was given evidence in the trial as well.

As Lieut. McNealy Mark's defense attorney called one of the witnesses for the defense. The witness for the defense was Carl's father Charles.

The defense attorney Lieut. McNealy asked Carl's father, "What do you think, Sir of Captain Mark's actions when it comes to this unorthodox rescue operation?"

As Carl's dad took the stand for the defense he said, "Now I know that what Captain Mark has done might have been wrong, however, thanks to Mark's actions a lot of people in this room have their husbands and father's back. Now I have served in the U.S. Army National Guard for many years, ladies and gentlemen, and of course, there is always something to say for our national security. However, when we leave men to rot in a foreign jail because it's just convenient for us to do so because these men may know something that our United States citizens should know and the taxpayers should definitely know how their tax dollars are being used to protect them. I think in my opinion we lost our democracy if people like Captain Mark and the rest of his crew put forth what they have done. But at least I know that Mark's actions have brought my son and all the crew back. Now, in my opinion, which in this case may not mean much, I think that Mark is a hero in this case. But I know that you people in this courtroom already have predetermined Captain Mark's verdict, and that is all I'm going to say about this."

After two days of trial, the trial has concluded. The next day came the sentencing.

The judge asked the jury, "Has the jury reached a verdict in the case of the United States Government versus Captain Mark Wrobel?"

"Yes, we have, Your Honor," The jury foreman answered.

"What are your findings?" the judge asked.

The jury foreman said, "We, the jury, find Captain Mark not guilty of all charges and he can be reinstated to active duty, whether time permits in this case."

The entire room erupted with applause as I stood up to hear the verdict with my defense attorney. I really had to sit down because I was so overwhelmed with emotions and I was grateful for the support that everyone showed.

After a few months after the trial, I officially retired from the military and the CIA.

ABOUT THE AUTHOR

Mark Wrobel resides in Wilmington, Delaware, and was born with a disability. But it didn't allow that to stop him from excelling in life. His father raised Mark; he was a dedicated single parent. He grew up in a communist system. Because of his disability, his country would not allow him to attend school with regular kids, but he persevered. Fortunately, when he was about 10 years old, he came to the United States, which he knew was the land of opportunity. So, he took full advantage of it and made sure he got a good education.

From 1989 until 1993, he attended St. Thomas The Apostle School, a Catholic school in Wilmington, Delaware.

Then in 1993, he attended Wilmington High School and graduated in 1997 with a high school diploma.

In 2002, Mark attended Delaware Tech Community College to attend their Web Designer Certificate Program, which he completed.

He continued his education in 2008 at Strayer University, studying Information Systems and Homeland Security. Mark graduated from Stayer in 2012 with an associate degree.

In 2018, he returned to Strayer University to obtain his Bachelor of

Science Degree in Information Systems and Homeland Security Management and graduated in 2020. He is proud of this accomplishment because he was told that it was impossible and he couldn't do it.

Mark is currently employed with the United States Coast Guard in Communications. He began working for the Coast Guard in 2012. Thus far, he has received multiple awards and accolades for his dedicated service. Mark loves to learn and try new things.

In 2007, he decided to try skydiving, and with the help of an instructor; he jumped 18,000 feet. There was an article published about it in the News Journal.

In the future, he would like to go back to school to obtain his master's and a doctoral degree.

Mark is the author of the titles Progressive Credentialism Versus Ageism, The American Holocaust, Start of the Coming Civil War, Unknown Secrets of World War II, and The Fall of the American Empire, which is available online worldwide. This is his sixth book titled Operation Wrath of Saladin and he couldn't have done it without his father's support.